WHITE HEAT
WHITE ASHES

WHITE HEAT
WHITE ASHES

TED SIMMONS

Tallahassee, Florida

Inquiries should be addressed to:
CyPress Publications
P.O. Box 2636
Tallahassee, Florida 32316-2636
http://cypresspublications.com
lraymond@nettally.com

Library of Congress Cataloging-in-Publication Data

Simmons, Ted, 1937—
  White heat, white ashes / Ted Simmons. — 1st ed.
    p. cm.
  Summary: Following his arrest on suspicion of arson, sixteen-year-old Pete is practically kidnapped by a white-supremacist group while seeking the friend who could clear his name, then tries not only to help rescue his friend's sister from the compound, but to undermine a second hate-crime, as well.
  ISBN 978-1-935083-00-9 (trade paper)
  [1. White supremacy movements—Fiction. 2. Hate crimes—Fiction. 3. Prejudices—Fiction. 4. Racism—Fiction. 5. Arson—Fiction. 6. Texas—Fiction.]
  I. Title.

PZ7.S59187Whi 2008
[Fic]—dc22

                    2008020311

ISBN: 978-1-935083-00-9

First Edition

Dedication

In loving memory of my Uncle Lou, and for Aunt Freddie, whose steadfast love has been like a quiet pond in a turbulent landscape

CHAPTER 1

I AWOKE TO THE NOISE OF THE FIRE ENGINES—heard the grinding of gears downshifting for the turn off Main Street, heard the pitch of the sirens drop as they sped north on the highway. I tried to fight the sense of panic sirens in the night always bring. For a brief moment I was eight years old again, and fire engines were converging on my house, while my father lay on the floor of his den in a pool of blood. I shivered under the covers, willing myself back to the present. I wondered if Mom was lying awake in her room, feeling the same cold sweat, the same fluttering in her chest.

It sounded like four or five separate engines, or maybe some were police cars—something big, for sure. I dragged myself out of bed and spread the slats on the blinds. I thought maybe, just maybe, I could spot a faint glow in the northern sky. Something orangey and flickery, not the steady yellow of the street lamps. I decided it was just my stupid imagination and threw my body back in bed, bouncing my head into the headboard.

Now I was really disgusted. No way was I going to get back to sleep again. The clock on my night stand said 4:08. Four in the morning! Crazy time for a fire. It was a thought I was going to remember the next day, when rumors of tragedy spread through the hallways and into the classrooms of Bennington High.

The rumors themselves were like a firestorm, creating a draft that magnified their effect. Or so I thought. Being a world-class cynic, I was sure the story had been blown way, way out of proportion by the time I'd heard it. It was said two people had been trapped inside a burning farmhouse. Within minutes, the number of victims had become three and, tragically, only one had managed to get out of the building. The truth, in the form of a statement from a grim-faced Bennington Police spokesman, was even worse.

Jennifer and I watched the television on the little wheeled cart that had been installed in a corner of the school library. Principal Hyatt—despite his being totally out of synch with anyone under thirty, and though he hated like hell coming into actual contact with anything so gross as a student—had a few good ideas every once in a while. For instance, he was big on keeping us plugged into world affairs. Whenever there was what the TV people called "breaking news," several sets would be placed at strategic points around the campus and turned on so his flock could gather and become "part of an informed citizenry."

The police officer on the screen stood with a microphone shoved in his face by a young female reporter. Behind them was a smoldering heap of blackened timbers.

Jennifer gripped my hand and a surge of heat, unrelated to the scene in front of us, flushed through me. I squeezed back, then forced my attention back to the screen.

". . . and we just don't know yet. A neighbor says a family of six lived in the house, farm workers. We aren't certain, but think they were all in there—a mother, a father, four . . . children." The officer choked up then and closed his eyes. The reporter started to say something but thought better of it. The cameraman, also recognizing the dramatic opportunity, panned in for a close-up of the officer's face. Tears could be clearly seen coursing down his leathered cheeks.

When he spoke again, his voice cracked. "We believe that . . . there is no evidence a single one of them, adult or child, managed to escape."

"Thank you, Officer Ferguson," the reporter said, as the camera moved back to reveal a third person, standing to her other side.

The reporter, oozing somber sincerity, spoke directly to the camera to tell viewers she also had with her Captain Frank Barnes of the County Fire Department.

She turned quickly and thrust the mic into the fireman's face. "What can you tell us, Captain Barnes, about the cause of this tragic blaze?"

The captain coughed a couple of times and rubbed his hand on his throat. He said, "Until we can enter the remains of the building for a detailed examination, it's too early to come to a definitive conclusion as to the origin of the fire."

"Isn't there evidence that this blaze was set deliberately, Captain?"

"There are certain suspicious items that must be checked, yes."

"I'm told," the reporter persisted, "that several gasoline cans can be seen around the periphery of the house. Are those the suspicious items you're referring to?"

"The presence of accelerant containers is always viewed with suspicion at the scene of a fire. But as I said, we can make no definitive conclusion at this time."

The reporter turned back to the camera, which zoomed in on her face. "So there you have it, live from the scene of a terrible tragedy that has occurred in this bucolic rural setting, just north of the town of Bennington, Texas, a normally quiet town, a town whose citizens awoke this morning to the harsh wail of sirens, and who have yet to understand the full extent of what has happened here."

With an exaggerated trilling of Rs, she signed off with, "This is Arrrrianna Lopez, Channel Three News."

Jennifer and I filed out into the corridor with several dozen classmates. No one spoke. From far down the hallway, normal sounds of lockers clanging and the banter of students who hadn't heard the broadcast made the silence right around me even more creepy.

Finally, Glenn Owens spoke up. "Joe Moreno wasn't in class this morning."

Someone else said, "Neither was Maria. I think that's his sister."

"You don't suppose they . . ."

It got quiet again. I didn't really know Joe or Maria Moreno, wasn't sure I'd recognize them if I bumped into them in a doorway. It was just someone's guess they were in the fire, but now those who died weren't just "victims"—they were real people. Those of us who'd been together in the library clung together like a litter of newborn kittens desperate for comfort and warmth.

I needed to talk, though. My head was so filled with thoughts and emotions, I thought I'd bust open if I didn't let it out. With a jerk of my head, I motioned Jennifer to follow me out into the patio off the lunchroom. We sat on a concrete bench and rested our elbows on a gray concrete table. Underfoot, gray concrete paving stones stretched unbroken to the surrounding walls, except for a few places where anemic palm trees were allowed to poke through. It seemed like the perfect place for the mood I was in.

I told Jennifer how I'd gotten goose-bumps hearing the sirens that morning in bed. "I know it's stupid, but I can't help it. There'd been all kinds of sirens that seemed to come to our house from all directions after . . . after my dad died. Ever since then . . ."

"It's been eight years, Peter."

"I know. It's stupid, but I can't help it. 'Course, I get over it a lot quicker now. Talk myself out of it, I guess."

"But it's still there."

"Oh, yeah. Every once in a while, like when I heard the sirens this morning, I'm eight years old again. I'm back in his den . . ."

"Stop it, Peter."

". . . in the room that was his little hideaway place at the end of the hallway."

"Quit now."

"I'm seeing the gun lying there, him on the floor behind his desk, in a pool of . . ."

Jennifer reached over and grabbed my hand again, and I stopped talking. One touch and wham, the past was gone. It was like that with her. Every part of me was right there in the courtyard on a concrete bench with Jennifer James.

I stared at her. How can I be so lucky?

When Mom and I had moved to Bennington midway through my sophomore year, friendship with the likes of Jennifer had been way beyond anything my little brain could foresee. Hell, I'd made no actual attempt at making friends with anyone at the school. I worked with kids on the school paper, the *Bennington Blade,* ran track with a few guys, got along okay with the brainy types, but kept to myself as much as possible.

My only real friend was Jerrod Wilson, who latched onto me for some strange reason, even though we're about as opposite as you can get. He's a bit on the chunky side, while I'm tall and skinny, wondering when I'll fill out so I'm not all elbows and knees. Jerrod's impulsive and gets into all kinds of trouble, leaping before he looks. I, on the other hand, tend to study things to death before I can do a damned thing. I make lists.

But I'm trying. I have to look good for Jennifer.

We'd been together in Chemistry class for six months before I actually talked to her, I mean, really talked to her. One afternoon she'd watched me being tormented by the testosterone crowd during an especially painful volleyball game from hell. She called me up into the bleachers afterwards, and I'd almost refused, certain she was going to rub more salt in my wounded pride. Instead, she told me how much she admired my stoicism.

"You were so brave," she said.

"Huh? If I'd laid a few of them out on the deck, maybe. But I just stood there and took it."

"If you'd have tried to fight them, that wouldn't have been brave. It would've been stupid. And stupid's one thing I know you're not, Peter."

I fell in love with her on the spot.

Sitting with Jennifer in that concrete courtyard, watching her hair bounce as she nodded at every dorky thing I said, I wondered again how this incredible female could have fallen for a guy like me. They say miracles don't happen anymore. I beg to differ.

"Hey, Pete." It was Jerrod, calling from the doorway. "Whatcha..."

I turned in time to see his eyes shift from me to Jennifer, then back. He dropped his chin on his chest for a sec, then looked back up and gave me a weak smile.

"Hey, Jerrod," I said. "C'mon out."

"I think not. Maybe some other time. I wouldn't want to disturb y'all or anything."

"We're just talking."

"Yeah, right."

"Get your butt out here."

"I'll pencil you in for later. Can't interrupt your talking."

When Jerrod had left, Jennifer said, "He's jealous of me."

"C'mon. Why would he be jealous of you?"

"I can tell, it's like . . ."

"You're crazy."

"You're blind."

"I mean, let's face it, you and he are two different things."

Jennifer laughed.

"Totally different," I said.

She laughed again. "Let's just say he's jealous of the time you spend with me."

"It's still dumb."

"God, you can be so obtuse, Peter."

"Obtuse?"

"Yes, it means you're . . ."

"I know what it means. It just doesn't apply. I'm not obtuse, I'm just right."

"You're always right. Never wrong."

"I know what I know. How can . . ."

There was a touch on my shoulder, and I whirled to confront Mrs. Larson, my English teacher and faculty advisor for the school newspaper. She flinched before I could get rid of the scowl on my face.

"Peter, I'm sorry to disturb you. Principal Hyatt would like to see you in his office."

Jennifer and I looked at each other.

Mrs. Larson seemed flustered. She went on. "I was there to talk about the *Blade*. There are some stories that . . . well, anyway, I said I'd come and find you. It took a bit of doing."

"Why didn't he just wait till next period, when he'd know exactly where I was?"

Mrs. Larson raised her hands, palms upward, and shook her head.

"He could have used the P.A.," said Jennifer.

"He felt it best not to . . . oh, just run along, Peter, run along."

As I left the courtyard, I looked back. Jennifer was staring at Mrs. Larson. Mrs. Larson was clasping her hands together in front of her chest and staring after me.

I was still halfway pissed at the idea Jerrod would be upset I was seeing Jennifer. I'm still his best friend. What's the big deal? I haven't changed. I was trudging down the hallway toward the front of the school when I had another thought. What if Jerrod has changed? It wasn't just Jennifer, but other things—little things that seemed different. He was too quiet. Usually Jerrod found life a perpetual joke he could laugh at. Lately, he'd been even more serious than me, no mean feat.

In the reception area outside the principal's office, a secretary I hadn't met was shuffling papers around on her desk. She looked up.

"Peter, is it? Peter Grayson?"

I nodded and tried to smile. She didn't give me back anything even remotely like a smile, and mine collapsed like someone let the air out.

"Just go on in. Mr. Hyatt is expecting you."

I opened the door and walked into the principal's inner sanctum. He wasn't at his desk, but seated in a small wooden chair. It had been pulled up to a coffee table centered on a large oriental rug in the "visitors" part of the room. He got up when I walked in, but I barely noticed. Instead, I was watching the two police officers who had been seated on the couch on the far side of the table. As they got to their feet, grim-faced, one of them said, "Mr. Grayson?"

"Yes?"

They walked around to where I was frozen in the doorway.

"This here is Officer Deakins, and I'm Officer Prescott. We're gonna have to talk to you, but not here. You're gonna have to come with us."

I must've looked dumbfounded, or just plain dumb, because he repeated everything.

"You have to come to the station with us. Now. There are things we'd like to know. Things we all need to know. Things we expect you to tell us."

CHAPTER 2

MR. HYATT SAID HE'D ALREADY PHONED MY MOTHER, and she'd meet us at the police station. Oh great! Mom worries like hell if I stub my toe. What's she making of this?

I couldn't figure out what I should be making of it, myself. My mind was whirling with possibilities, but nothing made any sense. If Mom or someone else, Uncle Tyler maybe, had been hurt, they'd have just told me, instead of this "things we have to know" bit. I decided to quit thinking and just wait—not an easy thing to do.

At the police station, we didn't use the front door where the general public goes in and out. Instead we went in a side door used by the police and others who worked there. I guess the reception desk and the communications center were up front, because the only sign of life at the side entrance was a young cop with short-cropped hair, doing paperwork at a small desk. He tensed as I walked in, but relaxed when he saw Prescott and Deakins behind me. He nodded at them and glared at me.

We walked down a poorly lit, gray-green hallway past several closed doorways to an open door spilling a bright rectangle of light into the hall.

Officer Prescott grunted something, and I looked back to see him jerking his head toward the doorway. I went in, and my mother dove across the room from where she'd been pacing. She grabbed my arm.

9

"Peter, what is this? What's happened? Are you all right?"

No hand on her hip, no accusing look, no, "Peter, what've you done?" Instead, my mom said, "Peter. Are you all right?"

"I'm fine, Mom. I'm fine." I looked at Prescott. "I think."

Prescott cleared his throat and said, "Mrs. Grayson, why don't you sit here at this table. You too, son."

We sat down, and Prescott took a chair, too. Officer Deakins continued to stand in the corner, like a statue. So far, he hadn't said a single word.

Prescott said, "Now, I don't want you saying anything until I'm finished telling you what we have. After I do, I'll read you your rights and make sure you understand you don't have to say a thing without a lawyer."

I was really scared now. It sounded like they were arresting me for something.

"But I don't . . ."

"Just hush till I finish, boy."

My mother took my hand and gripped it hard. She seemed more frightened than I was, if that was possible.

Prescott said, "We know, for sure now, the fire out at Epstein's farm was arson. Those people in that there house were murdered, plain and simple."

"Oh, how awful," said Mom. "Those poor people."

"It was pretty damn bad, yes, ma'am," said Prescott. "Not only had they set fire to every corner of the house at the same time, but they'd made sure no one could get out. The doors'd been wedged shut."

Mom drew her breath in, but didn't say anything.

"Why am I here?" I asked in a small voice.

"Just a minute." Prescott got up and left the room.

Officer Deakins continued to stand in the corner with his arms folded across his chest. I wanted to scream at him to say something, do something, but he just stood there. He wasn't even looking at us, for crissakes, just staring at a spot on the floor.

When Prescott got back, he placed a small box on the table. "Go ahead, look in it. Tell me what it is."

I leaned toward the box slowly, like cobras were going to leap out at me. The only thing inside was a small plastic bag, which looks like the kind Mom uses for leftover vegetables. I looked up at Prescott and shrugged.

"Well, take it out, boy. Take it out. It ain't gonna bite you. Just don't take it out of the plastic bag. It's evidence."

My hands shook as I lifted the bag out. I heard another sharp intake of breath from Mom.

"Where'd you get . . ." I stammered.

Mom cried out and grabbed her cheek with one hand.

Officer Prescott sat back. "Well, well."

I finally managed to say, "Where'd you get these?"

"I think maybe it's time for that Miranda statement now," said Prescott. "Wouldn't want some smart lawyer . . ."

"My son," said my mother, "my son has done nothing wrong." She drew herself up and punched out every word, hard and strong. I'd never heard her like that before. "Forget your Miranda. You can forget your lawyers and you - can - answer - my - son's - question. Where did you get those medallions?"

Prescott backed up again, like Mom's words were beating at him. He glanced quickly at Deakins, still being invisible against the wall. Prescott cleared his throat dramatically. Then he leaned forward and fired back at Mom. "These Nazi medals, along with that there little tag that says, 'Property of Peter Grayson,' they were found at the scene of the fire, ma'am." He said, "ma'am" really loud. "A specially nasty fire that was deliberately set, ma'am. It seems your precious son, Mrs. Grayson, is up to his eyeballs in something like we've never seen around here, leastwise not in my lifetime."

Mom didn't flinch a bit. "The Peter Grayson on that name tag is not my son."

"Oh, come now, Mrs. G, it's a bit late for that. I saw how y'all reacted when you saw the medals."

"The medals are his, yes," said Mom, "but the tag belongs to his grandfather. His name was Peter, too. The medals are souvenirs he picked up during the war. A war he fought against the Nazis, by the way."

During all this talk, my mind was working like crazy, trying to figure out what to say or do. I supposed they'd eventually have to take my mom's word I'd been home all night. But how was I going to account for the fact my medals had shown up at the fire? People knew about them. Somebody'd probably already pointed the finger at me, or I wouldn't be here. How else would they know to come looking at Bennington High just a few hours after the fire?

I decided to say something before I was asked.

"I took those things to school a couple of weeks ago. To show people in my Social Studies class. They got stolen."

Mom looked at me like I'd grown a second head. "Peter, why didn't . . ."

She shut her mouth then, like a trap, but not before Officer Prescott noticed what she was saying. He smiled one of those big, crocodile smiles that makes a person want out of the water in a hurry.

"I was ashamed to tell you," I said. "I was careless, left them after class. When I remembered to go back, they were gone."

"Should be easy enough to check that story," Prescott said. "Give me the name of the teacher who was in that class."

Now I was really in trouble. Truth was, I'd told a lie, and then another one to cover the first one. Now I had to dig even deeper into my imagination to come up with something else. I could feel sweat from the small of my back creeping down the crack in my ass.

I stood up. "I've got to take a . . . got to go to the bathroom. Bad."

"To the right. Second door," said Prescott.

Escaping into the hallway, I realized the wooden statue of Officer Deakins had moved! Not only that, he was following me down the hall. Jeez, is he going to come into the john with me?

When I busted into the men's room, I didn't take any chances but headed straight for one of the stalls and locked the door behind me. Deakins stayed out in the hallway.

I didn't really have to go, but I sat on the edge of the toilet seat. Time to think and think hard. I hadn't done anything wrong, but still, I couldn't tell the truth, not the whole truth. At least not till I'd had a chance to check some things out. God, what a mess.

Thinking's not much of a problem for me. I can think of a gazillion answers to any of life's little situations. The problem is choosing one of the answers. Half the time, before I get around to doing that, someone else steps in and acts. I'd gotten into some scrapes recently that needed some quick thinking, and somehow, my mind had come through. Would it bail me out of this one?

After I figured I couldn't stall any longer, I flushed the toilet and stepped out to wash my hands. Officer Deakins stuck his head in the door, and I'll be damned if he didn't actually talk. "You all right, kid?"

"Yeah. Just nervous, I guess. Affects my stomach." Not a true statement—nothing ever affected my stomach, but it seemed like a good thing to say.

When we got back to my interrogation room and Officer Deakins had gone back to imitating a statue, I sat down and tried to act cool, something I definitely was not.

"Afraid you won't learn a thing from my Social Studies teacher," I said, without waiting for Prescott. "It wasn't in her class I left the medallions. It was in the Math class before, and I never showed the teacher. Or anyone else. I took them out of my backpack intending to show them to people, but then the bell rang. I left 'em sitting on the edge of my desk."

Prescott glared at me, but didn't say a thing.

"Sorry," I added.

He shook his head, then waved me off with a backward flip of his hand.

Just then a man burst through the doorway, and we all jumped.

"Mark!" Mom said. It was my mother's boss, Mr. Langer.

He gave me a not-too-friendly glance, then went to Mom and put his arm around her shoulder. She shrugged him off. "You shouldn't have come."

"I heard Peter was in trouble and just wanted to help." He reached out toward her, with a pleading, sick-puppy look on his face. She pulled back again. Langer turned away from her and gave me a disgusted sneer.

I managed to pull my mind off my troubles for a minute and sneer back. I knew it was unfair of me to resent my mom getting back in the relationship game, but this guy Langer turned my stomach. He was not only a businessman but a politician who'd do anything to win people over. I'd seen him switch on the charm when Mom walked in, then switch it off like a light when she left. For me, he didn't even pretend any friendship. I was just a piece of garbage he was going to have to smell until I could be shipped off to college—or Afghanistan.

I'd been trying to get Mom to wise up for months, and it finally seemed to be working. She pushed the chair back from Officer Prescott's interrogation table and stood up. Her voice was hard. "I'm quite sure Peter and I can handle this ourselves—Mr. Langer." It was Mr. Langer this time, not Mark.

Langer glared at Mom and went to the door. He turned back and said, "Suit yourself." Then he was gone.

Officer Prescott sat quietly for what seemed like ages, then he waved the back of his hand at me. "Get out of here. I don't buy your fishy story for shit, excuse me, ma'am, but your ma here swears you were at home all night last night, so there's not much I can do unless we get more evidence."

As Mom and I left the building, this time by the door in front where her car was parked, Officer Prescott put his hand on my shoulder and half turned me around. "This don't mean you're off the hook, kiddo. I'd advise you not to try anything funny. I don't want you leaving town now, you hear?"

Leaving town? I'm not quite seventeen, I've got $87 in the bank saved up from mowing freaking lawns, and he thinks I'm going off to Bolivia or someplace?

The next morning I hadn't even gotten in the door before people were giving me cold stares and walking wide circles around me. Apparently, news of my "arrest" had made it around school while I was still at the police station. I was so shaken, I wanted to bolt for the door.

"Jaynine." I stopped a girl in the hall. She tried to go around me, but I stood my ground. "Where's Jennifer?"

She shook her head and tried to get by. I grabbed her arm and said, "I need to talk to Jennifer. Where is she?"

"Hey, Grayson, get your grubby hands off her." It was Dick Walters, one of Bennington's footballers. I thought he was a jerk just about any time, but now . . .

"Yeah, back off, buddy, we don't need your dirty paws all over our girls."

This time the speaker was Chris Eversol, and this time it really hurt. Chris was on the school paper with me, not best buds, but sort of friends anyway, or so I thought. I wanted to run.

"It's not true," I stammered. "Whatever they're saying . . . not true."

Now I did take off. Not running, exactly, but the next thing to it. I was almost to my first class when I saw him at the end of the hall. Jerrod.

I pulled up, then started toward him. Jennifer could wait. My Math class could wait. Anything and everything could wait until after I'd talked to Jerrod. I had to know just why the World War II souvenirs I'd loaned to my best friend Jerrod had come to be found where two adults and four children had been killed—murdered in the most gruesome way I could possibly imagine.

CHAPTER 3

WHEN I GOT TO THE END OF THE HALL and turned the corner, all I saw was another hallway. Jerrod had vanished. I know he'd seen me coming. We'd looked right at each other as I bolted toward him, but he'd spun around the corner anyway. Now he was gone.

I checked the three rooms along the way to see if he'd ducked into one of them. Two were completely empty, and the third was a music class filled with students bumping and scraping around trying to get their instruments out of their cases and into a little semi-circle of chairs. No Jerrod.

The only remaining door was the one at the end, which led outside to the parking lot. To make it to that door, Jerrod must have really sprinted. I tried not to think what it all might mean, but I couldn't help it. Jerrod was acting guilty as hell. It didn't make any sense. I knew him. He was my best friend. He couldn't have had anything to do with killing those people. I knew him. I walked down to the door and looked through a little window, but only for a second. I didn't even bother to push the door open and step outside. If Jerrod wanted to get clean away, and it seemed he did, he'd be long gone by now.

Did I really know him? Hadn't I just been thinking yesterday, before all this stuff hit the whirly-blades, that he seemed different? I hadn't heard one of his stupid jokes in weeks, and I hadn't

16

tried to tell him one of mine—it just hadn't seemed right. Jennifer thinks it's her. Is it? I shook my head.

But now . . . now I was starting to wish to hell it was just her and not something worse.

Somehow, my worrying about Jerrod helped me get through the day. People went on staring and walking big circles around me, but I kept my head down and did what I had to do. If a teacher asked me a question, I'd answer it. Otherwise, I sat still, waiting for the class, for the day, to be over.

After school I started to walk home. Usually I either took the bus, or hitched a ride with Jerrod in his bright red Firebird. When he'd first gotten it, I don't know whether I was more jealous of the car, or of the fact Jerrod had a doting father to give it to him. Either way, I got over it, sort of, and was happy enough to tool around town in the passenger seat.

As I suspected, there was no red Firebird in the parking lot. And there was no way I was going to ride the bus home this day. I hitched up my backpack, tightened the straps, and started to jog. My room at home seemed pretty inviting.

After I'd crossed Main and was heading up Austin Road, a dark blue car coasted by from behind, moving slowly. I caught a glimpse of faces staring at me from open windows, and I turned my eyes away, not breaking stride. The car, though, an old Chevy, pulled over to the curb in front of me and stopped. Three doors opened, and three guys got out. They stood on the sidewalk and faced me.

Damn. There was nothing to do but stop. It'd be chicken to run—and stupid, too. Fast as I was on the track, I was loaded down with a heavy backpack and I was already half winded. I stopped in front of them and waited for whatever was going to come.

What came was the middle guy's hand. He was holding it out, wanting to shake!

"Hey, Pete. Don't know if you know me. I'm Mitch."

I just stood there, not moving.

"Mitch Clauson."

I still couldn't think of anything to say. I was still trying to figure out what was happening. I stuck my hand forward a little, and Mitch grabbed it and shook.

"You know Erich? Zane?"

Each in turn held his hand out, and I gave them a little wimpy up-and-down that seemed to suit them fine, too. Mitch was clearly in charge, and Erich and Zane were along for the ride. Zane even seemed a little embarrassed.

Finally, I found my voice. "I guess I've seen you around."

I had seen Mitch for sure and maybe the one called Erich. I wasn't sure about Zane. Mitch and Erich could have been brothers. They both had really light brown hair, cut so short I could see the bumps on their heads. Zane's hair was cut the same way, but it was darker, darker even than mine. They each wore tight, straight jeans and white tee-shirts with pockets. It seemed like a kind of uniform.

"We've seen you, too." It was Mitch again. "Want to get a burger or something?"

I shook my head. I really didn't want to go eat with these guys. They weren't the jocks I'd had run-ins with in the past. They weren't jocks or brains or part of the rah-rah cheerleader bunch. They weren't Black or part of the Hispanic crowd that ate lunch together, speaking Spanish like it was some other country. They weren't anything. They were outsiders who kept to themselves. "Nah," I said. "Got to get home. My mom works, and I've got things to do"

"I like that," said Mitch. "That's good. Guys should help their parents."

I couldn't tell whether he was serious or putting me on.

"Trouble with the world, all these kids just care about dope and screwin' around," he said. "Good you're not like that."

I still couldn't tell if he was acting or being straight, so I said, "That's me, goody-two-shoes."

"Hey, that's funny, Pete. Goody-two-shoes. I'll have to remember that one."

I was embarrassed now. I stammered, "It's an old saying I read somewhere."

"Sure you don't want that burger? Zane here could use a smart guy like you around. He's missing a few things between the ears. You know?"

It was Zane's turn to go red. He stared at his thick, scuffed brown boots.

The one called Erich spoke up. "Lucky what he's got between his legs makes up for what he's missing 'tween his ears."

Mitch laughed, and I joined in, nervously, glad to know someone else was the butt of the joke, not me. For the first time all day, I started to relax a little.

"Hey, hop in." It was Mitch again. "If you won't let us buy you something to eat, the least we can do is drive you home."

Here were three guys making a real effort to be sociable on a day when my only friend turned his back on me, and the rest of the world seemed to hate my guts. I got in the car.

Mitch insisted I sit up front with him. As we drove, Erich stuck his head over the seat between Mitch and me so he could listen close to what was being said.

"So what about this fire thing?" Mitch asked.

Here it comes. "What about it?"

"What do you think about it?"

"It was pretty bad," I said. "Terrible."

"People think you did it."

"I didn't."

"Yeah, we know."

I looked past Erich to Mitch, who was staring straight ahead.

"How would you know?"

He didn't answer for a minute. One of his tires had a flat spot, and I listened to it flumping on the pavement. Then he gave me a quick glance and a quick smile and said, "Because you're not the kinda guy who'd do that."

This was getting weirder and weirder.

"You don't know me. I could be a serial rapist or a . . . or an assassin or anything."

I got quiet again, then said, almost in a whisper, "Everyone else thinks I did it."

Erich spoke up. "Jerrod doesn't."

Mitch flung his right back, and Erich had to push back in a hurry to keep from getting smacked in the face. Mitch's mouth was all screwed up in anger. He started to say something to Erich but changed his mind and forced a smile back on his face.

"Yeah, that Jerrod," he said. "Jerrod says you're a good guy. We believe him—no matter what all those assholes at school think."

"You know Jerrod? You've talked to him—today?"

Mitch threw Erich a dark stare that said, "Stay back there where you are." To me, he said, "Well, not today. But we've talked. I know a lot about you. Know about how your dad ate his gun, how you . . ."

"Jerrod told you about my father?"

"Well, yeah."

"He had no right . . ."

"Hold on, old buddy, hold on."

"Screw you, Mitch. And screw Jerrod, too. Stop the car."

"Cool it, Pete. He didn't mean no harm. He just . . ."

"Stop the goddam car!"

Mitch started to pull over to the curb, then sped up again. "I said I'd take you home. I'm takin' you home."

I pushed back against the seat, folded my arms across my chest, and stared straight ahead. Every once in a while Mitch looked over at me quickly, then back at the road. Erich or Zane coughed, and Mitch tossed another scowl at the back seat.

Mitch said, "C'mon, old buddy, lighten up. Even if Jerrod gave you the shaft, that don't mean we did."

"Don't 'old buddy' me." I was still hacked, but I could see his point. I added, "We're not buddies yet."

Mitch laughed then. "Okay. Okay. We'll give it time."

When I walked into the house, Mom was in the kitchen sitting at the table watching the door.

"What are you doing home?" I asked.

"I got off work a little early. I was worried about you."

"So what's new about that?" I started for the hallway leading to the bedrooms.

"Peter, please. Come and sit. Don't run off. I need to . . ."

"You need! How about me? I need to be alone. By myself."

"Peter." Mom's voice hardened. She pointed to the other chair. "Sit. I'm not asking, I'm telling. Sit down. We're going to talk—and now."

I threw my backpack on the floor and myself into the chair, making it screech back along the floor. Even as I was doing it, I realized how childish it was to act like that, but I couldn't help it. I was mad, I was confused, and I guess I was scared, too.

After a long silence, Mom said, "Have you calmed down, now? Can we talk?"

I nodded, but didn't say anything.

"Was it so bad today? At school?"

"They think I had something to do with the fire."

"Who does?"

"Everyone. Every stinkin' one of them. The whole school."

"But why would they?"

"Because somebody spread it around about my gettin' hauled in by the cops, that's why."

"But the police let you go. I told them . . ."

"That's right, you told them. You're my mother, they expect you to protect me. You heard that cop, that Prescott guy."

"Well, you were home. And that's that. They're the ones who have to prove you weren't."

"Tell that to the kids at school."

"Why didn't you tell me about losing the medals, Peter?"

"Like I said, I was ashamed."

Mom shook her head. "No. There's more to it. There's something you're not telling me."

I stared at the surface of the table and let my eyes trace the patterns in the wood. I should tell her. About Jerrod. About loaning him the medals. About him running from me today. About everything. Keeping it all to myself was killing me.

I said, "That's all there is. It's like I said."

She just looked at me.

"Sorry," I added, getting up from the table.

Mom stared after me while I stooped down to grab my backpack and headed out the door. She didn't say a thing.

In my room, I threw myself on the bed, face down. My chest hurt, there was something gigantic stuck in my throat, and I was millimeters away from crying. Why had I done it? Why had I lied again to the person who would always stick up for me? Why was I protecting a so-called friend who'd betrayed me, blabbed dark secrets about my past to strangers, run away from me just hours before?

I turned over on my back and watched a tiny spider hoping to establish a home in one corner of the ceiling.

Stupid spider. You'll last about a day in my mother's house.

I guess I fell asleep, because when I looked for the spider again, it was dark.

CHAPTER 4

ENNINGTON, TEXAS, ISN'T A BIG CITY, but it isn't exactly a small town either. Some people, especially those who live out on farms and ranches, talk with a real Texas twang and wear cowboy hats and boots and stuff like that. A few of the guys who dress that way—well, you know they're just city people trying to look "country." A lot of the people in Bennington are from somewhere else, like Mom and me—a lot of them not even from Texas.

We'd moved to Bennington from Connecticut at the insistence of an old friend of Mom's who'd come here years ago. Sarah had been working on Mom for a long time, telling her it'd be good for the two of us to get away from the place where such bad things had happened. Mom had fought it for years, insisting it would be worse for me to leave all my friends. Truth was, we could have stayed in Connecticut or moved anywhere in the world. It wouldn't have made a friggin' bit of difference to me. I'd have felt just as worthless anywhere. When your dad pushes and pushes and pushes you away and then goes and kills himself, it takes more than a change of scenery to make things right.

Here we were, almost nine years later, and I'd just about decided maybe I wasn't a total loser after all. I'd found a good friend, Jerrod, and then Jennifer. But now—everything was starting to come apart. Jerrod was gone, who knows where—or why. With all the rumors floating around, I needed Jennifer to reach out and touch me, but I just couldn't tell her the whole truth, any more than I could tell Mom. Maybe it was stupid, thinking I should protect Jerrod even if it meant holding back on people I loved, but I had the feeling I was being noble. I felt guilty as hell, but that was how it was going to have to be.

It was Saturday, thank God, and I holed up in my room.

Halfway through the afternoon, I heard voices out in the front of the house. Mom was talking to some man. A few minutes later, someone was rattling my doorknob.

"Hey, kiddo. Get your butt out here."

I ran to the door and jerked it open.

"Uncle Ty!"

"Whoa. Thought we'd done away with the 'uncle' bit."

"Ty!"

"That's better, kiddo."

"Suppose we could do away with the 'kiddo' bit, too?"

"Dunno. Someone of my advanced age has to maintain his dignity with you young-uns."

"S'pose you're right. You're a whole ten years older'n me. When you're eighty, I'll be just seventy. I'll still be able to take you in a quarter mile and have time to stop for a burger on the way . . . just like now."

"You won't have teeth for a burger. You'll be slopping oatmeal and soft-boiled eggs."

"We'll be feeding you through a straw. Or a tube."

Ty laughed. Then he pulled back and looked at me a long time.

He shrugged and held out his hands, palms-up.

"You don't look so bad. Your ma said you looked like hell."

"You came all the way over from Tallahassee, Florida, 'cause Mom said I looked bad?"

"Well . . . not exactly. She called to tell me about your brush with the law. I decided to make the trip."

"Just like that. You took off work and everything?"

"It's Saturday."

"Yeah. I forget when I'm having fun."

"Besides—can't have my favorite nephew being harassed by the coppers, can I?"

"They were okay . . . considering they think I'm a murderer or something."

"It's the guys at school that've got your jockeys in a twist, isn't it?"

"I guess."

I went over and sat on the bed and stared at my feet. I'd taken my shoes off, and I could see a hole in the toe of one sock. Better take it off before Mom sees it. I'll stick it on her sewing machine so she can fix it. I didn't move.

Ty didn't move or say anything for a long time, either. Then he came over and sat at the end of the bed and faced me.

"So, who is it that's giving you a bad time? Your big ol' uncle'll give 'em a thrashing."

"The whole school. Everybody."

"Teachers?"

"They look at me funny, but they haven't said anything. It's the kids. They make a big point of, like, walking on the other side of the hallway when they pass me."

"What about your girlfriend?"

"I haven't even seen her since it all happened. Nobody's been home. She said the family was going to spend a long weekend at the beach. Besides, what am I going to say to her? What's she gonna think when she hears all this shit going around about me?"

"If she really cares like you say she does, that's exactly what she'll think it is—a load of shit."

"I guess."

"Jeez, man. I've known you all your life. I knew you before this Jennifer came along, and believe me, if she sees something good in you, she's some kind of saint."

Ty put his hand on my head. "Bless you, my beloved, for even though you are a pitiful good-for-nothing slob, I, a saint, do find redeeming qualities somewhere in that demented soul."

"Spare me."

"I am Saint Jennifer, and you are the wretched cause that has led to my sainthood. Arise, my boy, and sin no more—or should I say spin no more." He spun around a couple of times, ending with a dramatic "tah-dah."

I sat with my chin on my chest, a twisted smile on my face, and my eyes raised up to watch him carrying on. All I wanted to do was lay around and be miserable, and here was my demented uncle making me smile.

"Okay. Okay. I'll call her tomorrow night, or if they're late getting home I'll see her Monday, if you'll just shut up."

Ty looked hurt, but you could tell he was pleased with himself.

"Now," he said. "What about your friend, what's-his-name?"

"Jerrod?"

"Yeah, Jerrod. How's he reacted to all this?"

"I dunno. When he saw me coming, he took off like . . . like the Roadrunner, or something."

"Bummer."

I sat quietly for a while, then said, "Ty?"

"Uh, huh?"

"I think there's a chance Jerrod had something to do with that fire."

"What?"

"I don't mean he set it or anything. It's just . . . I think maybe he knows something."

"Why do you think that?"

"I . . . I don't want to say why. Least ways, not yet. I wanna talk to him first." I snorted. "If I can find him."

"Okay. Have it your way. I'll be here tomorrow, too, if you need to talk. After that, you got my number."

"Thanks."

"What's a wise old uncle for?"

"There were three guys who stopped and gave me a ride home yesterday. Tried to be nice."

"There you go. It'll all work . . ."

"They make me nervous."

"Oh?"

"They're real weird. Loners."

"And you're not?"

"It's like they're a gang of loners, if that makes any sense. They look almost like skinheads."

Ty frowned.

I said, "They said they were sure I hadn't set the fire. Said it was good I was heading home to help my mom. Stuff like that. Really tried to be nice—at least I halfway think so."

"What's the other half of you think?"

"Dunno. Seems too good to be true, you know? Them comin' out of nowhere and trying to be friends, when everybody else is giving me the shaft."

"Having friends is good, but . . ."

"But what?"

"But, keep your eyes open, and your guard up."

"I will."

"I'll give you Unca Tyler's Second Law. If it's a choice between your brain and your gut, go with your gut."

I gave him a fake slug in his gut. He doubled up and howled like I'd hit him between the legs with a baseball bat. He was still hunched over and howling as he left my room.

I'd have liked to hear him explain himself to his sister, who had been banging around in the kitchen but was now quiet. I could picture her standing in the doorway with her hands on her hips, shaking her head at her little brother, or perhaps at the entire male half of the human race.

On Sunday afternoon, I worked up the courage to call Jerrod's home.

Mrs. Wilson answered. She wasn't her usual cheerful self. She sounded tired. At first I thought she was having trouble talking on the phone to a murder suspect. Then, I decided she was just . . . tired. She told me Jerrod couldn't come to the phone.

"I really need to talk to him, Mrs. Wilson. It's important. Please?"

She got quiet for a while, then said, "He can't come to the phone because he's not here."

"When do you expect he'll get home?"

"I mean he's out of town."

"Out of town?" I heard myself repeating what she said, like a stupid parrot. I added, quickly, "I mean, when'd he go?"

"Yesterday. He . . . went to visit his cousin, back east. He'll be gone a few days."

I hadn't heard about any cousins back east, but I guess that didn't mean anything. There were things about me I hadn't told anyone, even Jerrod. No reason he would have filled me in on all his distant relatives. Still—I had a funny feeling. I thought about Ty's Second Law. My brain said, "Listen to Mrs. Wilson. Believe her." My gut said something funny was going on. Go with your gut, Grayson, go with your gut.

Mitch Clauson caught me Monday morning before I even got to the front door of the school. Was he waiting for me?

"Hey, Grayson, how's it going?"

"Okay, I guess."

"Your ma okay?"

I dropped my eyebrows and tilted my head a bit. "Yesss . . ."

"Thass good."

He seemed sincere. This was just too weird. Totally beyond anything I'd run into before. Not that I was so worldly. Maybe guys did act this way. I just didn't know.

Keep your eyes open.

Mitch put his hand on my shoulder. I flinched but didn't pull away.

"So, I hope you're not still pissed your pal Jerrod told us stuff."

Keep your guard up.

"I guess not."

"That's great. It'd be a shame if y'all broke up your friendship, or something."

"Yesss . . ."

"Well, see ya around," said Mitch, giving my shoulder a squeeze.

Just like that, he was gone.

I wandered to my first class in a half-daze. I barely noticed people I passed in the halls, and have no idea if they were still acting like I had leprosy. I hadn't reached Jennifer the night before, and I needed to see her more than ever.

First period was Social Studies, and we were studying how the French Revolution affected the politics of the rest of the world. Usually, I'd be interested in stuff like that. I read a lot of history, and I like the kind that tries to trace how one culture leads to another and then to another. Or—going back the other way—to Rome and Egypt. What would a kid in ancient Egypt think if his best friend disappeared and his mother said he'd gone to visit a cousin in Mesopotamia or somewhere? What if some weird-looking guys with their heads shaved rowed across the Nile and tried to make friends—but he wasn't sure they were for real, or spies sent by the Pharaoh's evil minister?

I didn't have any classes with Jennifer that semester, so I had to catch her at lunch. We went back out to the gray concrete tables in the patio. There were a bunch of people already there, all of them girls, eating their lunches in the early spring sunshine. They were laughing and carrying on like the world wasn't falling into little pieces. It made me mad to see them enjoying themselves.

We got as far away from the giggling gaggle as possible. We sat facing each other across a table and didn't say anything for a while. I searched Jennifer's face for clues as to what she was thinking. She looked worried, but about what? Worried for me, or worried people might object to her sitting with me?

I finally spoke up. "Good weekend?"

"Pretty good."

"I tried to call you last night. Guess you got in real late."

"Almost midnight. Sorry I wasn't there when you needed to talk."

I stared at the ground a while longer, then said quietly, "I didn't do what they said."

"Of course you didn't."

"I was home in bed."

"I know."

"I heard the sirens, like I told you."

"Peter. Quit it. Do you really think I'd believe all the stuff going around?"

"Why does anyone think it? What've I done to people?"

Jennifer closed her eyes for a minute. Oh hell, here it comes. When she opened them up again, they were flashing with anger.

"You haven't done anything to anyone. People are just . . . cruel sometimes. They want to think bad about people. It's more exciting than thinking good."

"But why me?"

"Why not you? Look at yourself. You've made no attempt at being popular. You stick to Jerrod and me, and that's it. And if I'd left it up to you, you wouldn't even have me."

"That's not . . ."

"True? Oh, yes it is. You as much as said so yourself."

"I just never dreamed someone like you would . . ."

"Fall for a what? Say it. Fall for a loser like you?"

"Well, yeah."

Jennifer got up and walked around the table behind me and put her hand on my shoulder. I looked up to see the girls on the other side of the patio, quiet now, staring at us. I reached up and took Jennifer's hand and pulled her around to the bench beside me.

"Don't you see, Peter," she said. "It's the terrible part of human nature, when some people see a dog with its tail between its legs, there's an urge to give it a swift kick in the butt. You know?"

I nodded. I guess she was right.

"So I'm that dog."

"Until you think better of yourself, and make it clear to people you do, I guess maybe you are."

"Jennifer?"

"What?"

"You like me?"

"More than that. More than that."

"But why?"

Jennifer jumped to her feet and started to leave. She'd only gone a few feet when she turned back and said, "Because I'm a dog-lover, okay?"

Then she was gone.

I saw Mitch and his two buddies Monday afternoon after school. They were out in front on the sidewalk, standing in a little circle. Other people were having to walk on the grass or step off into the street to get around them, but they didn't pay any attention.

Whatever it was they were discussing had them agitated—or two of them, at least. Mitch and Erich were waving their arms around while they talked. Zane hung back and didn't seem like he was part of it.

I decided to hang back myself, rather than walk right by them. There were some flowering bushes along the front of the school, so I headed down the lawn, examining a couple of purple-pink blossoms that seemed to have gotten a head-start on spring. I was aware, even as I did, probably no other student in the history of Bennington High had spent any time studying the crepe myrtles.

I'd reached the end of the lawn and was turning back, when I realized the trio on the sidewalk had broken up. Mitch was heading for the parking lot, and the other two were going back into the building. They'd just about reached the steps when Erich saw me. He and Zane then came out on the lawn.

"Pete. Whazzup?"

"Not much."

"Guys still givin' you a hard time?"

"Not really. They're just not giving me any time. Like I'm not even here."

Erich said, "So get over it. I've been treated like that for years."

"It doesn't feel that great," I said.

"Who cares about all them bozos, anyway? Long as I got my buddy here . . ." He gave Zane a quick punch in the arm. ". . . what more do I need?"

"I don't even have that."

"Jerrod, huh?"

"Yeah. He took off. Blew me off like he never knew me."

Erich gave me a little, two-handed "who cares" gesture.

"His mom says he went to visit a cousin somewhere. I don't know why, but I don't believe her."

Zane and Erich looked at each other.

Zane spoke up, for the first time. He had a deep voice that cracked high every once in a while, like he was going through a late adolescence. He said, "We know where Jerrod is."

Erich whirled on him, then quickly looked around, guilty-like. I figure he was making sure Mitch wasn't nearby. Finally, he started walking back along the lawn away from the steps. He jerked his head for me to follow. He stuck close to the building. The crepe myrtles were already getting a little top heavy, and I had to duck my head a couple of times.

Erich got to a place where one of the bushes had died, and we ducked into the open spot. I thought if Erich wanted people to imagine we were doing something wrong, he couldn't have acted more suspicious. What is it with these guys?

"Zane wasn't supposed to tell you that," said Erich.

Zane said, "I just thought . . ."

"We're not supposed to think."

"You're not making any sense," I said. "Why shouldn't I know where Jerrod is?"

"You are—later, maybe. But Mitch says . . ."

"Mitch is your boss?"

". . . says not yet. He says after we get to know you."

"Mitch is your boss?"

"Not really, but . . ."

"But he makes all the decisions."

"Yeah, I guess."

"And you're just gonna leave me hanging. You know where Jerrod is, but you're scared of Mitch."

"Not scared, just . . ."

"Jeez." I shook my head.

I wanted to leave—get out of our little hiding place in the bushes and go. These guys were just too weird. But they knew where Jerrod was—or said they did. Wasn't finding Jerrod my first priority?

I leaned back against the building to think. I was being accused by practically everybody of being part of a crime that had happened while I was home in bed. Jerrod could have put me in the clear with one statement—that he'd borrowed my grandfather's Nazi souvenirs, so I couldn't have left them at the fire. But Jerrod had chosen to run, instead. Even more bizarre, Jerrod's parents seemed to be involved in it, too, giving me some hokey story about Jerrod going back east to visit a cousin. Then these two characters . . .

"What're your last names?" I asked.

"Scherer," said Erich.

"Weathers," said Zane.

I said, "Okay, Mr. Scherer and Mr. Weathers, tell your boss, Mr. Clauson, I want to see him."

"Whafor?"

"I'm going to ask him if he knows where Jerrod is."

"But we told you . . ."

"No, you didn't. I won't let on about what you've said. No sense Mitch getting pissed with you two."

The relief on Zane's and Erich's faces was pretty evident. I still didn't know what these guys were all about, but I knew one thing. Two of them, at least, owed me something.

CHAPTER 5

ITCH CAUGHT ME IN THE HALLWAY MIDWAY through the afternoon, and we agreed to meet after school. I suggested we go to the Dairy Queen, but Mitch didn't like the idea. "Place is full of assholes," he assured me. I didn't argue, even though the DQ was a place I'd spent a lot of time in myself, with Jerrod or Jennifer. "You know Buehl Park? The place where the band plays Fourth of July?" I did. "Meet me there at five o'clock. Okay?"

"Fine with me," I said. "Good a place as any."

"Yeah. Hope to keep it that way." Mitch walked off, leaving me wondering what he'd meant. Nothing came to mind, so I stuck it away in the back of my brain and got back to the problem of surviving the day.

Buehl Park is almost dead center in the middle of town. The City Hall and some other civic buildings are along one side of it. Some other big buildings, like banks, are on an adjacent side. Another side has large, old-fashioned houses with lots of fancy woodwork painted different colors. "Victorian," my mother explained.

The fourth side of the park, the north side, had a bunch of small stores, some of which had gone out of business. Drayton's Hardware and Kathy's Boutique were open, but I'd never seen anyone go in or out of their doors. They weren't even bothering to keep their storefronts clean. I supposed it was a matter of time before they tacked boards across their windows.

35

One place that definitely was still doing business was a bar. The Old Republic was always busy, with a stream of rough-looking characters going in and out all afternoon and evening. Some of them were biker types, others looked like farmers and ranchers— not usually a mix of people you'd see going in and out of the same establishment.

An alley ran from the square along the side of the "Republic." Even though it was narrow, I was standing in just the right spot to be able to see directly through to the next block. I started to turn away, but something in the alley caught my eye. Someone had come out of a door on the side of the bar and was looking left and right in the gloom of the alleyway. I wouldn't have given it a second thought, if he hadn't been so furtive. He walked toward the square and angled across the street toward the park. He was almost to the curb when I realized it was Mitch Clauson.

"You must have really good fake ID," I said, as he came near.

"Just talkin' to someone."

"Yeah?"

Mitch shrugged and sat down next to me on the bench, facing the bandstand. He didn't say anything for a long time, and neither did I. Then he pointed at the raised platform with the octagon-shaped roof. "Can you believe we've still got one of those?"

"Whatdya mean?"

"I mean, people come out here once a year and listen to old guys blowing on horns they had to dig out of a goddam closet."

"I think it's nice."

"Nice? Sure it's nice—used to be, anyway."

We both got quiet again. I couldn't figure out what Mitch was getting at, and he seemed to be off in space somewhere. Finally, he shook his head a couple of times and turned to face me.

"Erich said you wanted to see me." It was half statement, half question.

"Yeah. It's about my friend, Jerrod."

"Ah, Jerrod."

"The other day, in the car, you said you'd talked to Jerrod about me."

"Yeah, I thought we'd been through . . ."

"It's not that. It's something else. You tried to tell me you'd talked to Jerrod about me in the past, not recently."

"Yeah. True."

"But the things you talked about only made sense if you'd seen him after the fire. After I'd gotten hauled in by the police."

Mitch looked at the ground and scuffed a line in the dirt with the side of his shoe.

I went on, "So, I have an idea you know where Jerrod is. And it's not 'back east' where his mother said."

"She told you that?"

"Uh, huh. With some cousin I've never heard about."

"Cousin."

"I've never heard about."

Mitch gave off a low chuckle, so weak I could barely hear it. He said, also quietly, "I'll be damned."

"Is she wrong about that? Is she handing me a line?"

Mitch looked at me and gave me a crooked smile. He said, "Yeah, she's handing you a load of crap. Not sure why, but . . . yeah."

"So you know where he is?"

"Can't get one past you, huh, Pete?"

"Why would you . . ."

"Jerrod's out at the ranch."

"The ranch?"

"My friend Dwayne's got a place maybe forty miles outta town. Some of us hang out there."

"Including Jerrod? Why didn't I know about it?"

"Dunno. Jerrod just showed up Friday night. Said he wanted to see his sister. Then he stayed."

"Elaine? Elaine's there, too?"

"Yeah. She and Dwayne've got a thing goin', you know what I mean?"

"Are we talking about Elaine Wilson, Jerrod's snooty sister?"

"Ain't that what I've been saying?"

I got up and started pacing around, like a caged tiger just before feeding time. "And Elaine and this Dwayne fellow are . . ."

"Shackin' up? Yeah, sure. About a month now, I guess."

"Out at this ranch?"

"Like I said. That Elaine's some girl."

"You can say that again," I whispered, to myself mostly, for no reason I could think of. It was just something to occupy time while my mind whirled around.

"Several of the guys got their eyes on her, and I think she's eyeing 'em back—but Dwayne made it pretty clear."

"Clear what?"

"That anyone touches her, they'd better be prepared to lose the family jewels."

I laughed at his castration humor, because it seemed like what was expected, but, believe me, this whole conversation was very, very unfunny. We were talking about my best friend's sister here.

Of course, I'd never really liked Elaine. She always went around with her nose in the air, like she was better than anyone else. She'd had a succession of boyfriends she toyed with, then dumped when she'd gotten them all heated up. I, personally, would have run a hundred miles-an-hour the other way if she'd ever set her sights on me. Which, of course, she never did—and never would have. Her brother's tall, skinny, geeky friend?

Up till now, I hadn't known where I was going with this whole conversation, but things were pretty clear now. I had to see Jerrod. Had to find out what was going on. And to do that, I had to get out to this ranch.

I said, "So, how do I get there? To Dwayne's place."

Mitch stared off toward the "Republic." He said, "I dunno about that."

"Why not?"

"Dwayne's kinda picky about who he has out there."

I guess I lost my cool then. "What is it with you guys? I didn't come looking for you. You're the ones made a big deal about picking me up. Hell, I didn't even know you before that."

"We wanted to see what you was like. See if you was our kinda people."

"What?"

"You know. White."

"White? 'Course, I'm white. Just look at me."

"I don't mean on the outside. I mean on the inside."

I was starting to get the picture now. My Uncle Ty's warning about being careful with these guys flashed through my mind. There's trouble here. But I had to find Jerrod. Had to find him to clear my name. Clearly, I was going to have to play along with Mitch and his buddies—play some kind of role. But what? What exactly were they wanting me to be?

I said, "Sure, I'm white inside. Every bit of me."

Mitch scuffed at the ground again, thinking. Then he said, "C'mon. Let's go see Dwayne."

We crossed the street and skulked down the alley, checking to make sure no one was watching before we ducked into the side door. I felt like I was sneaking into an X-rated movie. I found we were in a short corridor that led into the back of the main part of the bar.

Even the darkness of the alleyway wasn't enough to prepare me for the gloom inside. The interior of the Old Republic seemed as dark as the corners of some Cretan labyrinth. No minotaurs lurked there, though. Only a bunch of tired-looking guys leaning on a long bar, and others sitting at tables around the room. Two of them were leaning forward, talking. Most were tipped back in their chairs with their feet stretched out in front of them. A couple had their heads back, staring at the ceiling, once in a while taking a drag on a cigarette and blowing the smoke straight up. The smell of the thick, noxious haze and stale beer was enough to make me gag.

Thankfully, I didn't have to put up with it long. Before my eyes had even started to adjust to the darkness, Mitch led the way through another short corridor past a bathroom that smelled so foul the smoke and beer seemed almost refreshing. We went out through a swinging half-door that looked like the saloon door from an old western movie.

Outside, under a green-and-white-striped awning, a small square bar surrounded a low cooler. A bartender was pulling out Buds and Shiner Bocks for a guy who'd elbowed his way between two older men sitting on barstools. They moved aside and went on about the serious business of drinking. Both the barman and the customer were young—if they were twenty-one, it was just barely. Both had ultra-short hair, like their heads had been shaved and new hair was just starting to grow out.

Mitch pointed to a red-headed man dressed in dark blue jeans and a new-looking jeans jacket, surrounded by three younger guys of the shaved-head type. He was pretty obviously in charge because they were all watching and listening to him and nodding their heads every once in a while. He broke off whatever he was saying when he saw us coming.

He gave me a grin that seemed impossibly large, but he hadn't been quick enough to cover up the look of irritation that crossed his face when he first saw Mitch and me. I have to admit, he threw it off well, because he leaped to his feet and stuck out a hand for me to shake, like he'd been waiting all his life to meet me.

"Hey, Mitch, is this . . ."

"Yeah. Like you to meet Pete Grayson."

"Pete, Pete . . . I'm Dwayne. Hey, have a chair."

Only one chair was empty, and it was at the far side of the table. I was just about to go around, when I realized Dwayne had jerked his head at one of the three young guys, who got up saying he'd see us later. Just then, the fellow who'd gone to the bar brought four beers and set them on the table. He was wearing what looked like old army fatigues. Something caught on my elbow, and I saw he wore suspenders hanging loose down his sides. A confederate flag flew on the sleeve of his jacket.

Dwayne said to him, "Why don't you take one of these, pick up a couple more, and you, Danny, and Chuck, head over yonder. I need to talk to Mitch and my buddy Pete, here."

A minute ago, he hadn't been quick enough to hide his irritation when I walked in. Now I was his buddy.

"Have a beer, Pete, Mitch."

I stammered, "I . . . I'm not . . ."

"Hell, man. Don't worry about that here. Look around. See any cops? See any windows with little old ladies snoopin' on us?"

All I could see were crumbling brick walls on all four sides of the courtyard and the underside of the green-and-white awning. I shook my head.

"So relax. Have a beer."

I took the beer, but I was hardly relaxed. I'd managed to wander into another world, right here in the center of Bennington—a world I hadn't even realized existed. Keep your eyes open, Pete. Keep your guard up.

"So, Pete," said Dwayne, "what you think about all these drugs around?"

Here it was. My interrogation. To see if I was their kind of guy. But what kind was that?

I decided, for this question at least, to tell the truth. "I wish they weren't."

"Why's that?"

"Because people get hooked and then go out and have to commit crimes to pay for more."

He seemed pleased with my answer, because he kept nodding his head up and down. Mitch was nodding, too.

Dwayne said, "You know where the shit comes from, don't you?"

"Colombia, I guess. Maybe Guatemala or somewhere like that."

"Bingo. And who uses it?"

"Lots of people. I know a bunch at school. Mostly marijuana, but some hard stuff, too."

"Sure, but it started in the big cities, don't you see? It's here in Bennington now, sure, but it started in the cities. In the parts of the big cities where white people don't live. Get it?"

I got it. "Yeah, it's a shame," I said.

"A damn shame. But it ain't too late to do something about it."

Mitch spoke up, then. "Jerrod's with us. How about you?"

I should have stood up and headed for the door. I should have jumped up and bolted for the out-of-doors as fast as my skinny legs would take me.

Instead, I took a deep breath, tipped the bottle toward Dwayne and said, "This is pretty righteous beer. American made for American men."

CHAPTER 6

IT WAS THE WEEK BEFORE SPRING BREAK. Every teacher seemed bound to send their charges off with memory imprints of exams designed to test the threshold of pain. For me, though, the whole school scene almost didn't register. Far from cramming, I barely gave the tests the benefit of conscious thought. Maybe my past sterling study habits carried me through, maybe not.

All I could think of was, I was deliberately getting involved with people who weren't just weird, but possibly dangerous. All their talk of "being white" was strange, but maybe the strangest part was I hadn't even thought about stuff like that before. Was I happy being a white guy? I guess, yes. Did I hang with any Blacks or Hispanics? Not really, not as friends. I'd taken three years of Spanish in school, and was pretty good at the reading part, anyway. Although I wasn't one of those who get all pissed hearing people talk Spanish to their kids in the supermarket, I figure those kids ought to be learning English, too, or they'd never cut it in this country.

On Friday, Mitch caught me in the hallway and said, "Tonight's the night, ol' buddy."

"What for?"

"You wanta be one of us, you gotta show your stuff."

"Stuff?"

"Yeah. You gotta show you're the kind of guy we can trust."

"You mean some kind of initiation?"

"Bingo."

"What do I have to do?"

"Can't tell you that. You gotta be surprised. You can get away, can't you?"

"I . . . I'm not sure."

"Just tell your mommy you've got important things to do."

I didn't know whether to be angry or ashamed, but tried not to show either. "You got a phone?" I barked at him. "I'll call you and let you know if Mommy will let me out of my playpen."

Mitch laughed and gave me his number. "You're okay, Pete, you're okay. I think you're gonna do just fine tonight."

When I got home, I took the phone into my room, closed the door, and called my Uncle Ty in Florida.

"Hey, what's up?" he asked.

"Don't get personal."

"Let me rephrase that. What's going on?"

"More of the same. Just wanted to talk."

"People still giving you a hard time?"

"Nah. Just ignoring me."

"Could be worse. They could be throwing rotten fruit at you."

"Or rocks."

"Stoning's sort of out of style right now."

"Uh, Ty . . . I found Jerrod."

"I didn't know you'd lost him."

"Maybe I didn't tell you. He disappeared last week. Made a big deal of avoiding me, then just took off. His mom said he'd gone to visit a cousin or something, back east. But she's lying."

"How do you know?"

"'Cause he's still here, or near here. On some ranch out of town."

"And . . . you know this . . . how?"

"It's those guys I told you about, who picked me up in their car. They've got this ranch, west of town. Jerrod's there."

Ty was quiet for a few seconds, then said, "My advice: Forget about it."

"That's what I'm thinking, too. They want me to go with them somewhere tonight for some kind of initiation."

"What?"

"They want to test me, to see if I'm their kind of people."

"You're not."

"A little bit of the stuff they say makes sense."

"Trust me on this, if they need to test you to see if you're fit to join 'em, you're not. Drop it."

"But I've got to find Jerrod."

"Why's it so important?"

"I . . . I still can't say, till I do find him. But trust me, I have to."

"So you're thinking to go with these guys? Play undercover cop?"

"I guess."

"Drop it, kiddo. You're not cut out for it."

"Why not?"

"Takes a special type."

"You mean I'm not brave enough?"

"Almost no one . . ."

"You think I'm chicken?"

"I didn't say . . ."

"Thanks for the advice, Uncle Ty."

I hung up.

At dinner, I was still halfway mad at my uncle, and angry at myself for being mad at him. After all, I'm the one who called him. If I hadn't wanted his opinion, I shouldn't have asked for it.

Mom was being as quiet as me. She was shoving peas around on her plate, so I knew she wanted to say something but couldn't find the words.

"What's up, Mom?"

She laid down her pea-pushing fork and put on a bright smile that looked forced. She said, "Mark wants to come by tonight. He says he wants to apologize for the scene at the police station."

I spun away from Mom, trying to hide whatever emotion showed on my face. What I felt was disgust.

"I'm afraid there's going to be a worse scene tonight," Mom said.

"I'll try to behave, but it won't be easy. I know you don't understand, but I really think I know the guy better than you. That sappy look he gets on his face when you're looking at him—the minute you turn your back, he gets a whole other look, and it isn't pretty. He looks at me like I'm dirt, probably because I know I don't fit into any plans he has for you two."

"You're right. I didn't understand. Not until the other day at the police station. Then I turned and caught a glimpse of the look he gave you. I felt cold all over. I never realized."

"I tried to tell you."

"I know. Guess I just didn't want to listen." She stared out the window. "It's been eight years."

"Mom, don't get me wrong. I'd like to see you dating again—and I don't need the speech about him not replacing my father. It's been eight years for me, too. But you deserve someone better than Langer."

She reached across the table and patted my hand. This time the smile was genuine.

I said, "So what about tonight? Why do you expect a worse scene?"

"Because I'm going to tell him I can't see him anymore, outside of work."

Alleluiah. "If it's okay with you, Mom, I was planning to go out tonight, but I'll stay if you need me."

She shook her head. "Thanks, Peter, but this is something I'd rather do without you here. I have some things to say . . ."

"Not fit for my tender ears?"

"Because I don't want to see you sitting there with an 'I told you so' gloat on your face."

In the car, Mitch asked, "Did you tell your mom where you were going?"

"No. Just said I was heading out to see some friends."

"That's good."

"She seemed happy enough."

"To see you go?"

"No. That I had friends to go off with."

Mitch laughed. "Well, ol' buddy, where we're heading, that's what it's all about. Having friends who'll stick up for you, no matter what kind of crap they throw at you."

"You mean all the kids at school, giving me a hard time?"

"I mean them, I mean the cops, the government, I mean everybody."

Up until last week, I hadn't had trouble with any of those groups. I had an idea some people joined gangs so they wouldn't feel alone and helpless in the world. But I'd never felt the need for anything like that. For me, it was enough for a friend to be just a friend.

I thought about Jerrod. What's happened to him? Why has he suddenly dropped everything, including me, to run with these guys? I hoped I'd be finding out soon.

We drove in Mitch's old Chevy to where the Brazos River made a wide loop around the eastern part of Bennington, before heading on south toward the Gulf of Mexico. As usual, I sat with Mitch, while Erich and Zane were in the back seat. Mitch parked in a little clearing below the highway bridge. There was one other car and a pickup truck already there. The only light was from a half moon and an orange glow from town, reflected off the bottom of some scattered clouds. They couldn't have chosen a spookier place.

I could hear the thump-thumping of cars on the bridge overhead, but this ordinary sound was hardly reassuring. Those people up there have no idea I'm here. They were going about their business, heading home from Burger King, going to the movies, picking their kids up from swim practice at the Y. But I was down here in the darkness, waiting for things to happen I didn't even want to imagine. Ty was right. I'm not cut out for this.

It was too late, though. I was here.

"Is it just the four of us?" I asked. Whoever had come in the other cars were nowhere around.

"No. There're others. Already there."

"Where?"

"Where we're going. Across the river."

"You're joking."

"Nope."

"Why didn't we park on the other side?"

"Not part of the deal. We use the railroad bridge."

We headed south on a path along the river, picking our way carefully in the moonlight. It was muddy in places, and my shoes were soon heavy with the gumbo clay that passes for soil in our parts. The air, too, was heavy with the smell of rotting vegetation and mold. At one point, the river bank dropped steeply, directly into the water, and we had to climb a slippery incline up into the trees. It really got dark then, but Mitch and Erich were prepared. They pulled little pen-lights out of their pockets, and we made our way through the woods.

"Watch the poison ivy," said Erich, shining his light on some triple-leafed viney bushes that seemed to be reaching out for me from the dark.

"It's all over the place," said Zane. "Gotta keep your hands up high."

Mitch turned off his light, and before I knew what happened, I bumped into him in the dark. He grabbed me and gave me a shove toward the dark green shrubbery. I fought to keep my feet, then realized he'd held onto me, and it was all a fake move. Very funny.

Mitch let go of me, switched on his light again, and laughed. "I wouldn't worry too much about poison ivy. There're worse things."

I wondered what worse things he had in mind, and whether they were waiting for me on the other side of the dark ribbon of water sliding silently beyond the trees.

When we reached the base of the railroad bridge, we had to backtrack away from the river to where we could climb up a gravel bank to the tracks. Mitch and I managed to sprint to the top in one easy motion. The other two slipped and scrambled on the gravel slope, using hands and knees as well as feet. We stood between the tracks for a minute to recover our balance. The dank odors of the river had been replaced by an oily, metallic smell, with every now and then a whiff of creosote.

"Okay, Grayson. Head on across the bridge," said Mitch.

"Aren't you . . ."

"Yeah, we'll be right behind you. Don't wanta miss the show."

"I don't have a light. You go in front."

"Nope."

"Then give me a light."

"Nope. This is part of what you gotta do. You chicken?"

Erich laughed. "Cluck. Cluck."

"Jeez," I said, and started down the tracks toward where the trestle's superstructure was a barely visible web of black against the faint glow of the sky. I couldn't see the ground, but I could feel where the gravel ended, leaving nothing but the crosswise timbers and the spaces in between them. They were too close together to fall through, but catching a foot and twisting an ankle was a real possibility. I slowed down and felt my way step by step. How often did trains come through here at night? At the rate I was moving, one was sure to come before I got all the way across. I remembered a newspaper article about two kids who'd gotten caught on another trestle across the Brazos. One had tried to run, the other had tried to cling to the side of the bridge. Both of them ended up in the river, dead. It took several days to find their bodies, way downstream.

Mitch said, "C'mon, Grayson. Haven't got all night."

"Screw you, Clauson. If I break a leg, it's you gotta carry me off of here." Anger was making me bolder than I normally would be. I was mad at Mitch, behind me with his flashlight, at Erich, at Jerrod. Most of all, I was mad at myself for getting into this stupid thing.

"I ain't carrying you nowhere. You break a leg, you crawl."

"I break a leg, you'd better take off the way we came. You try to get by me, you're in the river."

Mitch laughed, but I didn't join in. I hadn't meant it as a joke.

Someone said, "Damn. My ankle." It sounded like Zane, with his scratchy voice.

Erich said, "What happened?"

"Caught it in a crack. Whyn'tcha keep the light where I can see it, too, Erich?"

"You were supposed to bring one yourself. You can be so goddam stupid, I . . ."

"Don't call me that!"

"I'll call you whatever I want. Stupid."

"Stop it. Cut it out, Erich." Zane's voice rose an octave. He seemed younger, now. A little kid, out of control.

"Stupid."

"Shut up, shut up . . . shut up."

"Stupid, stupid, stupid."

"Both of you shut up." It was Mitch. "Concentrate on Grayson. Not on each other. Jeez."

Mitch's warning was too late, though. The spell had been broken. My fear had evaporated in the breeze. These guys might be weird, and a couple of them may be tough, but they were human, like me. I figured whatever they could dish out, I could take. I managed to get a feel for the spacing between the ties and picked up my pace. I'd show 'em. Of course, the bridge builders might've left a gap somewhere. I willed the thought out of my mind. I'd show 'em.

I glanced up and realized the dark lines of the trestle beams no longer framed the sky in a kaleidoscope of geometric shapes. Soon, I felt the reassuring crunch of gravel between the ties. I'd made it—with both legs intact. I felt I could accomplish anything. Bring on your silly initiation.

I said, "Now where?"

"Just keep going."

The rails were two thin, pale, silver ribbons. After five minutes of trudging along between them, I saw a flicker of lights through the trees to the left.

"Hold it." Mitch came up front with his flashlight and swept the bushes alongside the tracks. The ring of light settled on a barely visible opening and stopped.

"There. I'll lead the way now."

He stepped down the shallow bank and pushed his way through the shrubbery. I followed as close as I could so I could catch the bushes before they closed in behind him. I got whipped in the face a few times as a result. Erich followed me, and Zane brought up the rear. I figured Zane was having a far worse time than me, because he was keeping well behind Erich.

You could scarcely call what we were on a path. It was just a place where you could push the bushes aside and force your way through—if you could see them. From the train tracks, I'd seen the flicker of lights back in the woods. Now there was only darkness. If it weren't for the two tiny pen-lights carried by Mitch and Erich, I could easily imagine we were alone on the planet.

Mitch stopped and motioned me to come up beside him.

"This is where we go the next step," he said, pulling a dark cloth out of his back pocket. "Turn around."

"Oh, no. That's going too far." I stepped back, away from him. "You don't need that thing. It's dark enough in here."

"Sorry, ol' buddy. Part of the drill."

As Mitch fastened the blindfold around my eyes, the cocky feeling I'd discovered on the bridge disappeared in a flash. These guys might bicker among themselves like dogs in a kennel, but even fighting dogs will work together when they're chasing a rabbit. With his blindfold in place, the rabbit shivered, and the fur on the back of his neck stood up.

Mitch took my arm and started guiding me through the trees. Every time the smallest branch snapped back and hit me, I'd recoil, thinking I was about to get knocked flat. After a minute or so, we must have come into an open space, because Mitch pushed me along faster. When we stopped, he said, "Stand still."

"Are we there?" I asked.

"Just shut up and don't move."

I heard footsteps, the cracking of twigs. Then it got deathly quiet. Have they run off and left me here? Some kind of joke? I wondered how long I should stay, standing in the middle of the woods, in the middle of the freakin' night, blindfolded.

Then I heard whispering. A cough. From the cracks around the edge of the blindfold, I could see light. Bright light. A lantern, maybe? More whispering, then silence. By now, the hairs were standing up on my arms as well as my neck. I wanted to be gone. Anywhere. Anyplace but here.

Just as I was about to whip the blindfold off my face and make a run for it, I felt a touch on my chest, a light touch. A finger traced a figure eight around my nipples, up to my Adam's apple, and then down to my belly button, where it probed, lingering.

A low, seductive female voice said, "Hey, big boy."

Someone jerked the blindfold off, and I blinked in the sudden light. All around me, people whooped and hollered. It was all background noise, though, barely registering. All my attention was focused on the mass of blonde hair, backlit by lantern light, framing an almond-shaped face. As I stared, open-mouthed, the light was moved to the side. A small, straight nose came into view, along with a mischievous smile and sparkling eyes.

"So," she said. "Have a Bud?" She held the can out toward me, and I took it like an automaton. All my attention was on the giver, not the gift.

She laughed. "You don't talk much, do you?"

How could I, with my tongue stuck somewhere between my tonsils and my stomach? I blinked and swallowed hard, but I still couldn't say anything. I was still holding the beer can at arm's length, and she pushed it aside as she stepped forward again. She took my shoulders and turned me to the side, stretched her face up to my ear.

"I'm very, very happy you're here, Peter Grayson," she whispered, almost purred.

She nibbled my ear lobe, gave the side of my neck a little bite, and then . . . and then . . . she stuck her tongue in my ear.

I felt weak all over. The ground was melting away under my feet. All around me, the cheering ratcheted up a notch. It became a cacophonous din, a barrage of noise that threatened to flatten me.

I finally managed to force something through my constricted throat. I sounded like a strangled frog as I croaked, "I'm very . . . I'm happy . . . I'm . . ."

I settled for, "Me, too."

CHAPTER 7

ATURDAY MORNING WAS EVEN MORE OF a haze than the previous week. I stayed in bed long after waking up. I didn't want to face Mom's inquisition on why I'd come in so late, sneaking down the hallway in stocking-feet, knowing, even as I did, she was lying in her bed awake, fighting to keep herself from jumping up and nailing me on the spot.

As I lay there, I tried to separate reality from a night crowded with crazy dreams. What had happened in the woods? The trek down the river and across the railroad trestle—that'd been real, for sure. Thrashing through the trees, and the blindfold—certain facts. Carrie's tongue—Carrie Bell was the name she gave me afterward—must have been real. But I'd dreamed of that moment, and what came after, over and over throughout the night, so it was all a tangled mess of sights and smells and feelings. Feelings in every sense of the word.

The impressive quantity of beer I'd had sure didn't help. At first I didn't turn it down because I was too chicken. Later, it was because I was too sloshed to know what I was doing. Eventually, I was practically unconscious. The beer was another reason to stay in bed. I had a massive, pulsing, eye-watering hangover—something I'd read about but never expected to experience, at least not at my age. Hard to believe people do this on purpose.

Maybe scaring the hell out of me and then getting me drunk wasn't something my mom and teachers would approve of, but, aside from the hangover, I was finding it hard to remember why I was so suspicious of Mitch and his gang. Never in my almost seventeen years had any group of people taken me in so completely, gone to so much trouble to make me feel like one of them. And— since the whole party in the woods was for my benefit—not just one of them but someone special.

Jerrod had been there, beaming in the background like the Cheshire Cat. We didn't have a chance to talk, but once when I'd passed close to him, he'd winked at me. He's still my friend. It felt good, reassuring, to know I hadn't lost him, despite all the mystery of the past few days. Now, it seemed, I had a whole flock of friends, not just Jerrod.

And Jennifer, of course. Oh God, Jennifer. I felt a flush of heat and a sudden stab of guilt. Jennifer. How could I ever sit with her again in the courtyard at school, make plans, share a laugh at Principal Hyatt's latest act of stupidity? Jennifer, I swear, can take one look at my face and tell what I had for breakfast. How am I supposed to face her with the tactile memory of Carrie's fingers and tongue lodged in my brain, and a few other parts of my body?

It hadn't gone much further than biting and nibbling, or had it? Lying in bed with a head that felt like a machete-slashed coconut, I wasn't really sure. The night before, with the campfire, the beer, and the encouraging shouts of my new friends, I hadn't been stricken with bouts of virtue or thoughts about consequences. To be honest, Carrie could have taken me anywhere she wanted, and as far as she wanted to go. Maybe she did, and I just couldn't remember, the way I couldn't really remember them getting me home. The part of my body in question wasn't giving me a clue. My sheets were tented, and the tent pole felt like a Titan on a Cape Kennedy launch pad at ten seconds and counting. There was absolutely nothing unusual about that.

Not remembering what I'd done was scary. In addition to wondering who in hell Mitch and his gang were, I was beginning to question who I was.

"I was at a party. Sorry about being so late." I decided an up-front apology was the best way to deal with my mother—a sort of frontal attack to disarm her.

She was sitting at the kitchen table with the *Bennington Times-Sentinel*. The way she was holding the paper, it was apparent she wasn't really reading it.

She didn't say anything. I knew that no amount of toothpaste would cover the smell of liquor on my breath, so I kept talking. "There was some beer there. I'm afraid I had some." Some. Talk about your weasel words.

Still no response. Damn, she was good at this.

I said, "Did you buy Wheat Chex last time you went to the store?" I figured two could play this game. "I'd sure like some Wheat Chex."

Mom turned a few pages of the *Sentinel*.

"Yep. Wheat Chex is just what I need." I started opening and closing cupboard doors. Since I couldn't find any Chex, I settled on corn flakes. With the cereal in one hand and a carton of milk in the other, I nudged the refrigerator door closed with my knee and turned to face my mother. She wasn't there. During my little show of trying to act normal, she'd gotten up and left the room. Ouch.

The phone rang. I heard my mom answer, listen for a second, then say, "All right, I'll get him, if he's in any condition to talk." Ouch, again.

As I went into the family room to take the phone, Mom covered the receiver and said to me, "Says he's a friend of yours. He sounds as bad as you look." She left the room.

"Hello?"

"Pete, it's Zane. How ya doin' this morning?"

"Zane! You can guess."

"Yeah, I can. You were having a pretty good time of it last night."

"How come you're calling?"

"Truth?"

"Sure, truth."

"Mitch asked me to call you."

"And? . . ."

"And he wants you to go out to the ranch this afternoon. Can you make it?"

"No, I can't. It'll be weeks before things are back to normal with my mom. Think I'd better stick around and try for some damage control."

"Mitch says it's important. Says if you're Jerrod's friend, you'll come."

"What?"

"Said if you're . . ."

"I heard what you said. I just don't know what you mean."

"I don't either, Pete. It's just . . ."

"Mitch said."

"Well, yeah."

My new good feelings about Mitch started to wilt.

"What's he got on you? How come you ask, 'How high?' every time he says 'Jump'?"

"C'mon, Pete. Don't be that way. If it wasn't for Mitch . . ."

Zane quit talking, but it didn't take a genius to complete the sentence. If it wasn't for Mitch, Zane wouldn't have any friends at all.

"Let me ask you something, Zane. What do your parents think about Mitch and the other guys?"

"Mom doesn't give a damn about who I see." He was quiet for a few seconds. "About anything, really."

"And your dad?" I asked, knowing the answer even as I did.

"So who's got a dad?"

"You, too, huh?"

"I mean, who's got someone who deserves to be called Dad. Anyway, look." Zane's voice got hard, cranked up a notch and an octave, too. "Are you gonna come this afternoon or not? What do I tell Mitch? Yes, you're Jerrod's friend, or no."

Jeez. What could I do, with him putting it that way? I listened to hear if Mom was hanging around. She was in the kitchen, so I lowered my voice, sighed, and said, "Where at? Where do I meet you?"

When Mitch picked me up in front of my house, I immediately challenged him with, "What's this about Jerrod? If I cared about Jerrod, I'd come?"

"What are you talking about?"

"Zane said you told him to say, if I'm Jerrod's friend, I'd come with you."

"He probably got it wrong. Zane's not too swift, y'know."

"Seems bright enough to me."

When we picked up Zane, and then Erich, no one said a word about the way I'd been summoned. I decided to let it drop and sat back to watch the scenery as we headed out of town.

There was nothing marking the turnoff to where we were going except for a piddly little printed red-and-white sign tacked to a piece of weathered wood. It read, "Private Drive."

"What's the name of this ranch?" I asked Mitch.

Mitch did a one-finger spin of the steering wheel as he came out of the turn onto the dirt road.

"Dunno. We just call it the ranch."

"But it belongs to Dwayne?"

"Yeah. Or probably his mother—I dunno. The two of them live here—and the others. I guess you can call it the Nichols Ranch."

"What others?"

"We all of us stay out here sometimes. Some most of the time. Some come and go, like me and these two buttheads in the back seat."

Zane and Erich chuckled quietly, but didn't say a thing. I guess they were used to being the butt of Mitch's humor.

The gravel road twisted along a small, dry creek lined with trees, then headed across some plowed fields. Nothing was sprouting, so I couldn't tell whether they'd been planted yet, but the long, straight rows of dark soil were rich with promise. We came to a barbed-wire fence stretching as far as I could see in both directions. There was a chunk-chunk-chunk from the tires as Mitch drove over a cattle guard, not slowing at all. In less than a second, we went from domesticated farmland to the haphazard and unruly landscape of ranchland. Cattle country.

Bright green spring grass and clusters of scraggly oaks made the whole scene look peaceful and unspoiled. A good place to get away from people, I thought. A herd of cows huddled together under some oak trees, all facing the same direction, as cows seem to do. It seemed to me like a pretty good life, as long as you didn't mind going along with the crowd, and if you didn't know what was in store for you.

Only one thing marred the idyllic scene. Dark mounds of dirt dotted the pasture—a brown-on-green polka-dot pattern of fire ant nests. The nests were spaced almost evenly, like it was a master-planned ant community.

"Funny," I said.

"What's that?" said Mitch.

"I was thinking of Mexico City. Millions of people crowd themselves into slums, but here's a bunch of fire ants, smart enough to spread out. Make sure each nest has enough food."

Mitch looked at me, then shook his head. "You always thinking stuff like that?"

"I dunno. I guess. Why d'you ask?"

"No reason."

After another minute or so, Erich spoke up. "About those ants."

"Yeah?"

"They probably build their nests away from the others like that so they don't get stepped on by the cows."

I looked back at Erich in surprise. An original thought from a guy who didn't seem able to go to the bathroom without Mitch's permission?

I said, "Bet you're right. That, too."

Mitch spoke up. "People don't have to live in slums. I mean, look where we're heading. Lotsa people live off away from other people."

"Sure, but . . ."

"You know why?"

"No."

"'Cause the world is full of cows, and every one of 'em is trying to step on you."

"So Dwayne and you and the other people that hang out at this ranch—you're like fire ants?"

"You got it, man." Mitch was suddenly very angry. He pounded on the steering wheel as he spoke. "Try to step on us and we'll . . . we'll swarm the hell all over you. Give you some goddam bites you won't forget."

Whoa. I pressed myself back in the seat and tried to turn my mind away from Mitch and his hot-and-cold, manic-depressive psyche. I tried to concentrate on the scenery and wondered when I'd spot this ranch we were heading for, and why I was being summoned in the first place.

But now, with the cows and the fire ants whizzing by, I wondered again about what Zane had said to get me to come with them. There was no way Zane could have got it wrong. And he sure as hell wouldn't have made it up, not Zane. I figured maybe the answers would appear soon enough, as the road was making a beeline for a row of buildings just coming into view.

We parked in a dusty space surrounded by a barn, six or seven long porta-cabins, and a white two-story ranch house. As I got out of the car, the smell of dust and manure and hay hit me. Some chickens had fluttered out of the way as we drove up. Now they were pecking their way back to where they'd been, ignoring the new intruders.

There were eight or ten vehicles in the lot. All but three, a Cadillac Eldorado, a blue Buick, and Jerrod's red Firebird, were pickup trucks. Several were old and decrepit, others new and expensive. All of them were covered by a layer of dust from the road they'd traveled to get here. The truck nearest to me had two bumper stickers. One read, "Gun Control is Using Both Hands," and the other said, "Life sucks—just don't suck back!"

Mitch grabbed my arm and steered me toward the big house. To my left I could see several people coming out of the porta-cabins and staring at us. I got the impression that at least one of them was a girl, but Mitch was hustling me along so fast, I wasn't sure.

As we approached the house, a slight movement drew my eye to a set of windows directly over the front door. Someone was standing there, watching us. I caught a glimpse of bushy dark hair over a high pink-red forehead, a reddish nose and a dark mustache. He was wearing a short-sleeved dress shirt and a dark tie. He wasn't being sneaky, peeking through the curtains, or anything; he stood boldly in the window for a few seconds before he turned away. But behind him was another figure—the phantom silhouette of someone who seemed like he wasn't supposed to be seen.

Mitch opened a large front door, painted white like the rest of the house, and nudged me inside with a little push to the small of my back. Erich and Zane, as usual, trailed behind.

"Dwayne here?" Mitch called out, to no one in particular.

A woman with short, spiky, light brown hair came out of a side door. Behind her, I could see a room full of tables and desks, bookcases, and at least three computer monitors, casting bluish light. She was wearing jeans and a plaid shirt over a slim body that looked boyish. I figured she was maybe in her early twenties. She said, "He went to town. Hey, who's this?"

"This's Pete."

Mitch didn't introduce her, so she stuck her hand out and said, "Hey, Pete. I'm Amy. The smart one around here."

I said, "Hello. Glad to meet . . ."

"Yeah," interrupted Mitch. "She thinks she's the smart one, 'cause she knows all about that computer shit. She'd starve to death if she had to cook a meal, though."

"And you wouldn't?" Amy said.

"It ain't my job. We been through that before."

"Okay, Mitcheroo. The minute you qualify yourself to take over the web from me, I'll cook you a goddam meal. Or wouldn't that be man's work, either?"

Mitch was about to fire back, but broke off at the sound of a deep, booming voice from the top of the stairs. We all turned and looked up.

"Now I know why I only had one child of my own." The speaker was a large woman with graying red-brown hair, cut very short. She was dressed in something from a late-night TV rerun of *Bonanza*—brown skirt, brown denim shirt, brown jacket with fringes. It would have looked fine on a smaller, thinner woman, but this lady was big. I mean she was large in every direction—a Hoss Cartwright of a woman. Her voice was large, too, and swept like a stampede down the stairs.

"Maybe you two have forgotten. I'm the one who decides what's man's work or woman's work around here."

She started down the stairs, then abruptly stopped halfway, successfully defying the laws of inertia. "So this is young Mr. Grayson?"

I nodded, still a bit caught up in Mitch and Amy's verbal ping pong match and amazed by the sight of the apparition on the stairs.

The apparition let gravity take control again and resumed its descent. She was surprisingly graceful. Inertia is doing its job this time, I thought, keeping her from bobbing up and down at each step.

"Don't mind these two. Mitch is a dinosaur who thinks women should be restricted to the kitchen and the bedroom."

"Not true," said Mitch. "All I say is a real woman will include a little cookin' in the things she does—and as to the bedroom . . . same thing."

Amy snorted. "In your dreams, Mitcheroo. In your dreams."

"Hell, I wouldn't touch no dyke like you for . . ."

Amy lunged at Mitch and probably would have dragged him to the ground, if the female Hoss hadn't intervened. I couldn't believe how quick the woman was, jumping forward and grabbing Amy's wrist.

She held on to Amy, glared at Mitch, but spoke to me. "Sorry you have to see my children misbehavin' like this. It's not too likely either of these brats are gonna introduce me."

She pushed Amy away, then turned to give me her full attention. "I'm Beatrice Nichols, though folks around here call me Bea. Behind my back, they call me 'Aunt Bea,' but only behind my back, you understand."

I nodded, still not quite willing to trust my voice.

"I don't suppose you know why you're here, do you?"

"Something . . . something about my friend. But I still don't . . ."

"Truth is, you're here 'cause I sent for you."

"You sent for me?"

The big woman put her arm around me, and I thought I was going to disappear into a mass of buckskin. She swept me through a door and into a western-style living room, complete with a *Bonanza*-sized stone fireplace.

"Of course I sent for you. If I hadn't, you wouldn't be here."

"It was Mitch invited me."

Bea hooted and shook and slapped her knee. "Mitch's no different from any of the other inmates in this asylum. I'm the warden. I'm the CEO." She shouted out into the hallway, "I'm the head honcho here, and don't you forget it."

There was no sound from beyond the door. Either Amy and Mitch had left, or they decided silence was the best response.

Bea motioned me to sit on a couch whose frame was made of logs, painted white. The rough fabric had Indian designs—spirals and step pyramids and mythical stick figures—in different browns and yellows and tans, colors Mrs. Cooper had called "earth tones" in eighth grade Art. Bea settled her enormous bulk into an oversized chair that had to have been made especially for her. This was Mother Earth on steroids.

"So I'm not here because Jerrod needs me?" I said.

"Heavens, no. I've had little to do with your friend Jerrod. My son says he can be trusted, so I've allowed him to stay. Dwayne has his faults, but he's generally a good judge of character."

"Including mine?" I was starting to get my composure back, enough to ask some questions anyway—try to figure out what was going on. I wasn't prepared for Bea's next question, though.

"So, tell me, young Mr. Grayson, just how good is your Spanish?"

"Excuse me?"

"I thought I was speaking loud enough. Let me ask you again. Your Spanish. How good is it?"

"I . . . I dunno. Okay, I guess. I read it pretty well. Don't speak it very good, though, and I only catch a word or two from Spanish television . . ."

"Why did you decide to take Spanish?"

"I don't really know. I had to take some foreign language."

"You didn't have to take three years."

"Yeah, but I decided I liked it. And . . . how did you know I took three years?"

"How'd I know you took it at all? You were saying?"

"Well, it seemed like it might be useful."

"Because Spanish really isn't a foreign language anymore, is it? You hear it everywhere you go right here in America, don't you?" Bea's voice was rising now.

"I . . . I guess so. Sure, that's why I kept taking it."

Bea shook her head, slowly.

"Well, that can't be helped now. And besides, it's the reason I invited you here. I'm not interested in how well you read it or how you speak it. What I want to know is—can you write Spanish?"

"I suppose."

"Then, Mr. Peter Grayson, welcome to the ranch."

CHAPTER 8

THE BACK DOOR OF THE RANCH HOUSE HAD once opened up to the outdoors. A series of steps led down from a small porch with a low railing on the sides. It was now completely inside another building, however, which had apparently been tacked on later—a large open room with half-a-dozen tables, each with six chairs. Fans, hung from the high ceiling, turned slowly and soundlessly.

I heard the faint clinking and clanking of porcelain and metal through a door on the far side of the room. They were low kitchen sounds that made it seem even more silent where I stood on the little porch with Zane, who'd been charged by Beatrice with giving me "the tour." I looked over at him. Why isn't he saying anything?

I decided to speak up. "Dining room, huh?"

He shook his head and said, in his crackly voice, "Nah, this here's the mess hall."

I laughed. "Same thing."

"Just call it the mess hall, okay? We got words for things. Words's important, Mitch says." He glanced at me quickly and added, "So does Dwayne—and Bea."

Zane got quiet again. When I looked at his face, he turned his eyes away and stared at the row of windows along one side of the "mess hall." He wants to say something to me, but can't work up the courage. I could see a little twitch in one of Zane's cheeks. He was maybe a couple of inches shorter than me and not quite as skinny. With his close-cropped dark hair and smooth cheeks, he looked really young. Only his voice and a couple of angry red zits on his chin gave any clue hormones were coursing through this kid's veins.

Zane shook himself out of whatever trance he was in and stomped down the steps. He seemed to be angry. "C'mon, let's go. You gotta see the place 'fore mess call."

The smells of simmering beef and fresh-baked bread met me before we got to the kitchen door. Inside, four women were scurrying around, causing the clanking noises I'd heard faintly from the steps. From inside, the kitchen was filled with the sounds of silverware and plates being loaded onto trays, hissing and bubbling from several large pots on two stoves, and the banging of pans being washed in a deep sink. What I didn't hear was talking. The women were working, heads down, as if each was alone in the room, with an assigned chore to do. As I watched, though, a slender and tired-looking young lady poured the contents of one pot into another, then handed the empty pot to the woman at the sink, who took it without turning her head, and immediately started to scrub it. It's like a machine. A quiet, well-oiled machine.

All of the women had glanced up as we came in the room, but three of the four quickly went back to their work. Only one continued to watch us—a woman with a leathery face full of wrinkles and thin, wispy hair that flew in different directions even though most of it hung to her shoulders. I'm sure she was a lot younger than she looked. She had the kind of face I'd seen before on women who never seemed to be without a cigarette dangling from their lips.

Zane made a stab at introducing us. "This's Pete. And . . . Marty. This's Marty."

Marty stood with a hand on each hip, one of them clutching a dishtowel.

"Pete's new," Zane went on.

Marty snorted. "No shit. I'd never guessed."

Zane's face colored. I decided to step forward.

"Hi, Marty. Like Zane said, I'm Pete. Pete Grayson."

I've never figured out whether or not a guy is supposed to stick his hand out first to shake with a woman, but I did anyway. Something had to happen.

Marty didn't move. She looked at my hand, then back up at my face. After what seemed like forever, she nodded her head, and her cracked face broke into a grin. She slung the dishtowel over her shoulder and took my hand. "Well, well. What've we got here? Some kinda gentleman you've brought, Zane." She added in an exaggerated southern drawl, "Ah do declare."

Her hand was clammy with dishwater and cold, but it warmed up as she kept holding onto mine.

"Hey, ladies. Say hello to our young gentleman caller."

The two women at the stove turned and nodded their heads, but didn't say anything. The young, tired-looking one tried to smile. It seemed to be too much of a struggle, so she went back to stirring. The other one was probably older than Marty, but still nice to look at, with a short, neat haircut. She did smile, and said, "Hi."

The fourth woman looked to be the youngest of the bunch, but it was hard to tell because she kept her back to me.

"Well, it's been nice meeting you," I said, dropping Marty's hand and starting for the door. It was pretty obvious the "gentleman caller" had interrupted a routine that didn't take well to being interrupted.

I was halfway through the door when a familiar voice cut into my brain. I stopped and whirled. The fourth woman was facing me now with a scowl that would have shriveled the Pillsbury Doughboy. This was no woman, though.

"You asshole." She stretched the "ss's" out into a long, menacing hiss.

"Elaine!"

"First my busybody brother, now you. What the hell you think you're doing?"

"I don't understand . . ."

She turned away and started moving stacks of dishes again, muttering, "Dorkbrain. Nosy little bastard."

I started to object, to tell her she had nothing to do with my being there. After all, I'd been invited—by Beatrice Nichols, no less. I didn't finish the protest, though. It would've sounded weak, even to my own ears. I'd allowed myself to be invited—and for a lot of different reasons. One of them was the need to know why my friend Jerrod was there. The other was why Jerrod's sister Elaine was there, and just what she and Dwayne had going.

I started out the door again, but couldn't resist one parting shot. "Not to worry, Elaine. There's things—and people—even a dorkbrain wouldn't stick his nose into."

Zane herded me out a door at the side of the mess hall so we could continue our tour of the compound. Stretching in front of the door was a concrete sidewalk with narrow, branching walkways on either side, leading to a double row of porta-cabins.

"This's where we sleep when we're here," said Zane.

"Have you got your own bed? I mean, do you keep your clothes and things here?"

"Got a locker. But I use any bed's empty. 'Course, the staffers got their own beds and everything. They live here, so they gotta."

"How many staffers are there?"

"I dunno. Depends. 'Sides Bea and Dwayne there's . . . well, you met Amy when we come in, and Marty and Dutch and Francie in the kitchen. You know Elaine."

"Yeah, I do. How 'bout Jerrod? Is he a staffer?"

"Maybe. I doubt it. Bea's real big on kids finishing school, so after the break . . ."

"So that's it? Those are all the guys who live here permanent?"

"There's two or three more. We'll see 'em at dinner." He looked at his watch. "Which is in twenty minutes. We better get movin'. Bea don't let us eat if we're late."

We went into the last porta-cabin on the right. It was open inside—one large room with four beds, a table, and four chairs.

"This here's my bed this week. And that's my locker. That's mine all the time."

"Wow! Your own locker! That's sure decent of them."

Zane didn't seem to notice my sarcasm. He said, "And that's yours."

"What?"

"Your locker. You can bring stuff to keep in it. To use when you're here. They ain't givin' you no bed, 'cause you're supposed to just come here weekends. Bea wants you to stay in school, like me."

I dropped my head and put my hands on each side of my face for a second, then held them out, palms up. "What are you saying? The reason I'm supposed to keep going to school is because Bea, excuse me, Aunt Bea, says so?"

Zane just shrugged.

"And I'm supposed to come here whenever Aunt Bea wiggles her little finger, to write in Spanish or . . . or whatever the hell it is she wants from me . . . and I'm even going to get my own locker? Whoo-whee. I'm so excited."

Zane looked alarmed.

I headed for the door, saying, "C'mon. I think it's time I finished my talk with Auntie Bea."

"Wait! Wait, Pete." He clutched at my arm. "Please don't make no . . . don't make trouble for me."

I spun back, then stopped and watched Zane. He was scared as hell. He was actually shaking.

Jeez. What am I doing? If I'm going to find out about Jerrod, I have to stick it out no matter how weird things are. "Why would it be your fault?" I asked quietly.

"I dunno. 'Cause it always is."

"What if I leave you here. Go alone?"

"No. That'd be worse. I was supposed to show you around. I gotta do it. They said." Zane often acted and sounded even younger than he looked.

I shook my head. "Okay, Zane. You win. Go on back to being tour guide."

At the end of the double row of porta-cabins, the walkway turned left, then became a dirt path leading to the barn. Off to the right of the path was a low fence. Just beyond the fence were bales of hay lined up in a row. Across a field were more hay bales, stacked high. Attached to them was a large white poster with a life-size black silhouette of a man. Even from a distance, I could see a scattering of bullet holes.

We went into the barn through a side door, and my nose was assaulted by the smell of hay, manure, and animal sweat. Four horses were shuffling nervously in their stalls. The dark brown one nearest to me lifted its head high and stared sideways, with a lot of white showing in its eyes. It didn't seem all that friendly.

"Hey, Brownie," I said. Brownie gave her nose a couple of upward tosses.

"You any good with horses?" asked Zane.

Brownie and I maintained our wary eye contact. "Never been on one in my life. Maybe a pony when I was a kid. Don't really remember."

"Everybody here rides some. Bea thinks we . . ."

"Bea thinks everybody should ride, so everybody does."

"I guess."

"Even Mitch?"

"Yeah, sure, Mitch."

"Funny," I said. "Mitch is Dwayne's slave, Dwayne jumps whenever his momma Bea farts. Kind of a hierarchy of slaves."

Zane looked confused.

"You know, a pecking order, like chickens."

"I think we better get back to the house," said Zane. I think I'd strayed into territory he didn't want to be in, or else he still didn't have a clue what I was talking about. Here I go again with my big mouth. I'd better quit this smart talk. If I'm going to be their kind of people, I'd better act like it, even with Zane.

I shot one last look at Brownie, who chose that moment to give me a dismissive snort. I decided Bea'd have to command her slaves to lasso me and hog-tie me to the saddle to get me on one of those beasts.

"Better hurry," said Zane.

I figured Zane didn't need any trouble on my account, for his sake and mine, so I trotted after him out of the barn and across the parking lot.

As we neared the house, I glanced up at the window over the front door to see if the man with the mustache and the shadow man were watching again. They weren't. All I saw were thin sky-blue curtains fluttering in the breeze of another ceiling fan whirling beneath a white ceiling.

We walked straight through the house to the mess hall. Several people were sitting at one of the tables, and a couple more were coming in the side door as Zane and I started down the stairs. Two were women. Two were skinheads I'd first seen with Dwayne at the Old Republic Bar and later in the woods. Another was Jerrod. He nodded his head at me, or at least I think he did. It was just a quick shake before he looked away. I was sure he'd ask me to sit with him at one of the empty tables, but instead he sat at one that was already almost full. Zane and I sat by ourselves. After a minute, Mitch got up from the full table, came over, and joined us. Erich followed. So this is the way it's going to be. I'd been adopted by Mitch and his disciples, and dropped by Jerrod like a massive turd.

Zane looked toward the kitchen, then to the door to the house. He jumped up. "I gotta go to the bathroom quick. If the food comes, save me some, please."

When he was gone, I asked Erich why they kept Zane around, if they thought so little of him. Mitch spoke up. "Every team's gotta have a mascot, don't it? It's fun having him around."

"To pick on?"

"He don't mind. He likes it."

Zane came to the table, out of breath.

"You like it Zane. Don't you?" said Mitch.

"Huh?"

"Oh, nothing."

Marty was framed in the kitchen doorway, a dishtowel slung over her shoulder. She stood there, obviously waiting. Then she nodded to someone across the room and spun back into the kitchen. I turned to see Bea flowing down the steps in a sea of swirling blue fabric.

"My God," I said.

Mitch laughed. "Kind of a change from buckskin, huh?"

"You can say that again."

"Bea likes to surprise."

I said, "Looks to me like the same material as the curtains in the upstairs window, the one in front."

Erich said, "Yeah. Couple acres of it."

Mitch and Zane slugged him in the shoulder almost simultaneously. Mitch said, "Shhhh," and Zane said, "Jeez, Erich."

Like a large blue bat navigating by sonar, Bea wove her way through the tables and directly to ours. She put her hand on Erich's shoulder, but she spoke to me. "So, Peter. Here's what I'm expecting you to bring to our little family—a higher level of intelligence and better manners than we already have here. It shouldn't be too difficult." She gave Erich's shoulder a hard squeeze, making him squirm. Then Bea turned away and sat with Dwayne in the far corner, at a table set for only two. Mother and son sat facing each other and waited for their dinner, neither of them talking.

From the kitchen door, Marty and Elaine and the other two helpers burst into the room with trays loaded with food. They were amazingly efficient. In less than a minute, everyone was eating, and the kitchen help had retreated as quickly as they appeared.

I said, between mouthfuls of beef stew and hot bread, "Speaking of the curtains in the upstairs room, I saw some guys at the window. Just after we got here."

Mitch and Erich looked at each other. Zane stared at his plate.

"I don't see either of them now," I added.

"There's only one guy, but he don't eat with us," said Mitch.

I wasn't going to argue with Mitch. If the other guy hadn't wanted to be seen, chances are Mitch didn't know about him.

I asked, "So who is he?"

"Just a guy. Comes and goes."

"Just a guy? No name? What's he do?"

"We dunno. 'Cept this. Bea don't take orders from no one, but just him."

"What kind of orders's he give?"

Again, Erich and Mitch glanced at each other. Then Mitch said, in a low voice, "I think . . . maybe you need to be with us a while before we talk about stuff like that."

CHAPTER 9

FTER DINNER, I WENT OVER TO BEA'S TABLE to say good-bye and thank her for her hospitality. She and Dwayne were still sitting in silence. I'd been watching them throughout the meal, and I doubt they exchanged a half-dozen words the whole time.

"Thanks for dinner. Tell Marty the food was great."

"It always is. You can tell her yourself."

"Afraid I've gotta go. I had a hard enough time getting away. Mom's not too keen on . . ."

"This is the start of Spring Break. I thought maybe you'd stick around. Show us what you can do."

"Oh, no. Mom'd have fits."

"Not to worry. It's all taken care of."

"What?"

"I phoned her. Said you'd be staying with your friend Mitch and his family down by Galveston. Said it'd do you good to do a little swimming. Breathe the fresh sea air. She agreed."

"But . . . we're not anywhere near Galveston. I don't even know Mitch's family."

"Sure you do. We're his family." She pursed her lips and tilted her head back. "I stretched the point a little with your ma. Said I was Mitch's mother."

"But why? And why didn't you talk to me about it?"

"You were off with Zane."

"What I want doesn't count?"

Bea sat back in her chair. Her voice got hard. "What counts is that our work gets done. What counts for you is you do your part. It's what's done in a family."

"I still don't get it."

"Forget the 'I' business. It's 'we' here, not 'I.' Understand?"

I didn't say anything. Suddenly the whole summer camp atmosphere had dissipated. The soft, billowing folds of Bea's dress only accentuated the harshness in her voice and the menacing expression on her face. For a minute, I felt light-headed, like the room was spinning. I closed my eyes for a few seconds.

". . . in the morning," Bea was saying, "right after breakfast, see Amy. She'll tell you what to do." With that, Bea stood up, pushed her chair back, and hauled herself up the stairs, with considerably less grace than coming down. Dwayne stood, too, glanced at me with a weak smile, then walked around the table and pushed his mother's chair in place. Soon, like Bea, he'd disappeared inside the house.

I started back to the table with Mitch and Zane and Erich, then changed my mind and headed for the side door. I needed to be alone. Outside, the sky in the west was fiery orange. To the east, it was already looking dark. That was how I felt, half blazing mad and half frightened of the dark secrets this place held. I'd been disarmed by the party in the woods, by Mitch's attempt to make me feel welcome. For sure, he'd treated me better than he treated Erich and especially Zane. But why? I was beginning to think nothing around here was as it seemed.

Got to remember why I came. Have to keep my head. Gotta remember Ty's warning, "Eyes open, guard up." There was little chance I was going to forget it after the heavy-handed way Bea went about keeping me here. For chrissakes, I've practically been kidnapped!

I'd reached the end of the porta-cabin row and turned left onto the dirt path, when I heard someone behind me, running. I started to quicken my own pace, but looked back to see it was Jerrod, just turning up the walkway to one of the buildings. He stopped at the door and looked back toward the mess hall and the main house. There was no one in sight. Quickly, he whirled and continued to race down the path. He shouted, "Come on," as he rushed past, and I followed him into the barn.

"What the hell? What's going on?"

"I don't want 'em to know I'm talking to you. Not yet."

"Why not? We're friends. Or we were."

"Something's happened, and they're not . . . they don't know whether to trust me."

"What happened?"

"First, I gotta know why you're here. What'd they do to get you here?"

"They didn't do anything, except be friendly. You were at the party."

"Yeah, but why here?"

"They gave me this story about how I'd come if I was your friend. Then Bea said that was just horseshit—no offense there, Brownie."

For a second, Jerrod smiled. For a second, he seemed like the old Jerrod, but it was gone in a flash. He was worried, and it showed.

"So you came because of me?"

"Truth?"

"Sure, truth."

"Partly, it's 'cause I miss you, miss being friends with you. Partly, it's because I'm mad as hell at you."

Jerrod looked away.

"You drop me in deep shit with those medals you borrowed, then take off and let me get blamed."

Jerrod nodded his head, still looking away.

"One word. One word from you was all it would've taken."

"I couldn't. You can't understand."

"Jerrod, I dunno what's happened to you. But, jeez, man, I know you couldn't have had anything to do with that fire."

"You can't understand."

"Understand what? Try me, for God's sake."

Jerrod almost shouted. "It was either you . . ." Then he got really quiet. ". . . or Elaine."

A row of scraggly trees lined the course of a dry creek that wound through the pastures. Jerrod and I were meandering along a faint path between the trees and the dew-coated grass. We had agreed to meet the next morning before breakfast. It was barely dawn.

"Look," Jerrod was saying. "Whatever you do, you gotta promise me you'll help me get my sister outta here."

I huffed. "Elaine and I haven't exactly been *simpático*, you know."

"Yeah, I know she can be meaner'n a skilletful of rattlesnakes, but she's my sister. My folks are worried out of their gourds."

"They know you're here?"

"Sure as hell ain't happy about it, but they couldn't think of a better plan."

"Plan?"

"To spring Elaine before the shit comes down."

We walked on for a couple of minutes. The only sounds came from the cracking of twigs underfoot and the call of a mockingbird from a perch overhead.

"What time's it?" asked Jerrod.

"Seven-fifteen. About."

"Breakfast's at eight. We better start back."

"Tell me about the medals. And the fire."

"I wasn't there. I promise."

"The medals."

"Look, I'd been trying to buddy up to Mitch so's I could get out here to do something about Elaine."

"Yeah?"

"It wasn't working too good. He kept putting me off. I don't think he trusted me."

"Didn't think you were one of their kind, huh?"

Jerrod looked at me sharply, then nodded. "Exactly."

"So you had this brilliant idea."

"Uh, huh. I heard them talking about Germany before the war and the Nazis and how they'd been so misunderstood."

"Yeah, right."

"Well, then it clicked. I'd loan 'em your medals to soften 'em up. You know, get 'em to think I was 'one of their kind,' as you said."

"Jeez, Jerrod. Do you know what you're saying? You have knowledge—no, you have proof—of who set that fire at Epstein's farm. And instead of going to the police, you're here living with them."

"Don't you see? We had to get Elaine out of here first."

"We? Your folks are part of this! They know about the murders, too?"

"You don't understand. Elaine . . ."

"You don't want her charged with the rest."

Jerrod broke another long silence. "Besides we don't have proof of who set the fire. All we know is somehow the medals got there."

"Jerrod!"

"Huh?"

"I just had another thought. Why did the medals get there? And why were they left there, so the cops could find them?"

Jerrod looked at me, wide-eyed. "I just guessed it was a mistake."

"Fat chance."

'I dunno. Maybe one of 'em just happened . . ."

"Bullcrap. That box of Nazi medals was left there on purpose. And Jerrod . . ."

"What?"

"My grandfather's name, which just happens to be my name, was written on the box. I was set up. I was set up on purpose."

I found Amy already at work in her computer room. She greeted me when I came in, but with less enthusiasm than she'd shown the day before. It was time for business, it seemed, and time to act businesslike.

"Bea said you'd tell me what to do."

"Pull up a chair." She motioned to a table along the wall. "Here's what we need you to put into Spanish." She handed me a one-page typed message.

"I'm not all that fluent. I need a dictionary for some of the words."

"We thought of that." Amy took a paperback Spanish-English dictionary out of a bookcase and handed it to me. The spine had never been creased.

"Am I supposed to write it longhand, or type it, or what?"

"Type it, of course. It's got to be printed—and sent by email."

"I'd have to have a word processor that does Spanish. There's different letters in Spanish we don't have in English."

"Bull. I've seen Spanish. The letters are the same."

"Except you gotta put an accent mark over some letters or the words have the wrong meaning. Then there's the tilde over some of the Ns."

"The what?"

"The little wavy line that makes the N sound like it has a Y after it." I showed her the word, "señor."

"So leave it off. They'll know what you mean."

"I guess, but it'll come out stupid."

"So, who cares? The people that're gonna read it aren't all that smart, anyway."

"'Cause they speak Spanish?"

"Because they can't speak English. Don't be such a dunce."

"The morons probably can't speak Danish, either, or Thai."

"What?"

I figured this conversation wasn't getting me anywhere. And besides, if I was going to seem like one of their kind, I'd have to pretend to go along with their idiotic logic. "Never mind. You're right. I'll type it without the accent marks and the tildes."

"Use this computer. Hold on a minute. I'm in the middle of editing something."

She turned back to a television screen she'd been looking at when I came in, and turned the sound up. On the screen was a tape of a news program I'd watched with my mom the night after the fire at Epstein's farm. It had been big news that night, not just locally, but nationwide. No one had yet come forward and admitted responsibility, or rather taken credit, for the blaze, but the reporters said it had all the earmarks of one of those white supremacy groups that hang out in the back woods, as far as they can get from any sort of government.

The announcer was saying, ". . . and the dead, now believed to be six in all, were Mexican-American farm workers, parts of two families, employed by Paul Epstein, a Jew whose father escaped from Germany and came to America in 1938. Because of this, attention has focused on those militant groups who call themselves the Seedline Identity Movement."

The announcer then turned the program over to a militia "expert," who explained that, no matter how abhorrent the Seedline beliefs might be to ordinary people, the believers were absolutely convinced they were right.

"They are convinced beyond any doubt that the white race has a mandate from God to preserve its 'purity' from intermingling with darker-skinned people, who they call 'mud' people."

The Seedliners reserve their most venomous attacks for the Jews, who they claimed to be Satan's instruments, and responsible for almost every bad thing the world had to offer.

"The attack on Epstein's farm was no random act," the expert said. "It was a calculated and deliberate act of war."

"Goddam nonsense," said a Seedline spokesman. "This is another example of the (bleeping) government and the Jewish media trying to lay the blame on us again, just like they do to the Klan and all the good white organizations that are trying to do God's will. We don't need to kill us no spics. We don't even need to kill us no Jews. God'll take care of all that when the time comes. And you can believe your ass, that time is a-comin' soon, yessir."

It would have been easy to dismiss the man's words as the ranting of an illiterate fool, if it weren't for the cold sincerity of their delivery. His message was no casual letter-to-the-editor. It appeared to be a deep-felt belief that dominated his life. I wondered how a person could become so single-minded in hatred of other people. I'd never been able to figure out how people could let their lives revolve around any single issue. Why don't they get a life?

I studied Amy as she worked. Her face was tight with concentration. She obviously felt she had a life—one which made her feel important. Maybe that was the answer. Everyone wants to feel useful, part of something larger, a group.

I asked Amy what kind of editing she was going to do.

"Not much. Just going to get rid of the profanity bleeps. Don't want to detract from the message."

I turned to the paper Amy had given to me to translate. It was in the form of a business memo. The first part of it read:

To: The Spanish Speaking Peoples Residing in
          the United States of America

From: Soldiers of W.A.R., the White Aryan Resistance
Subject: Fair Warning

Be advised the time is fast approaching when decent
people (white) from all corners of this God-given land

shall rise up and depose the unlawful Zionist Occupational Government (ZOG), residing now in our nation's
capital. When this occurs, people of color and non-Eng-
lish-speaking peoples will cease to be given preferential
treatment and protection from ZOG.

It went on to say that W.A.R. had no quarrel with Mexicans or
Central Americans, provided they stay out of the United States,
which had been bestowed by God on English-speaking whites.

"How do we know this about God and the United States?" I asked
Amy, when she seemed to be taking a break from her editing.

"It's in the Bible, stupid."

I hadn't done a lot of Bible-reading since my dad died, but
during my Sunday-school days, I sure didn't hear anything about
America being mentioned in the Bible at all. It had already been
around a millennium or two in 1492.

"We'll be having lessons tonight," said Amy. "You'll see."

The document in my hand was chilling. Its purpose was to give
the Spanish-speaking people fair warning, so W.A.R. could not be
accused of being inconsiderate of people whom God had chosen
to be subservient to whites, "much like beasts of burden and the
flocks of the field." In spite of the contention it was being issued as
a kindness toward its intended audience, the message was clear,
and frightening. Get out of the country, or else.

I thought about something Jennifer had said about how people
can think things, even terrible things, if they only know part of the
story, but think they know it all. The most dangerous people in the
world sincerely believe they're right and everybody else is wrong.
Watching Amy calmly editing tapes and planning the distribution
of hate mail, I shuddered. I'd been brought here by these people
for a purpose, because of a minor skill none of them had. I'd been
stalked and caught and reeled in like a fish on a line.

Frightened as I was, the adrenaline rush didn't induce me to
either fight or flight, unless you could call putting myself into an
emotional coma a form of flight. I'm ashamed to say I seized on

the task I'd been given, and pushed everything else away. Truth was, I couldn't let Amy know how I felt—I couldn't even let myself feel what should have reduced me to a quivering mass of mindless flesh. Instead, I switched every one of my brain's synapses to the task of figuring out how to translate such phrases as "Zionist Occupational Government" into Spanish, using a $6.95 dictionary.

CHAPTER 10

A s I struggled with Spanish grammar in the computer room, I heard the front door opening and slamming repeatedly, and the noise of bantering in the hallway. One of the new arrivals stuck her head in the door and said, "Hey," to Amy, who waved her hand without turning from her computer screen. I looked up to see the back of a blonde head, just as it ducked back into the hall. Carrie Bell. She either hadn't seen me, or ignored me, I wasn't sure which. A stab of disappointment crashed like a wave dashing on rocks before draining slowly back into the sea.

More and more people arrived. Something big was going down. I wanted to see where they were all going, but one look at Amy's deep concentration discouraged me. Clearly, I was expected to follow her lead and "do my part for the family," as Bea had not-so-tactfully instructed.

It wasn't easy. As I'd feared, many of the words weren't in the dictionary—at least not in the sense they were meant. As I worked, I played around with the idea of changing the message to something less menacing. Maybe I could even make it friendly, or just nonsensical. These guys'd never know. Or would they? They didn't seem like a trusting bunch. They'd probably have some way of checking things. Even a crude, word-for-word eyeballing of the dictionary would catch any obvious attempts to fool them. I decided to do the best I could, without worrying about the finer points.

85

When I finished, Amy told me to save the file with the name, "Warning." She'd attach it to email messages. "I've got a whole mailing list ready to go."

"So, do you send it now?"

"Nah. Later, when Gaith . . . when Bea gives the word."

Just as I thought. They were not going to send the warning out until someone had time to check it and make sure I hadn't screwed them over.

When Amy and I went out into the hallway, the house was quiet. I stood at the bottom of the stairs and cocked an ear. No sound was coming from the upper floors. I glanced into the living room, but Bea's massive couch and chairs were empty.

We went back into the mess hall just in time to see the last of the group heading outside. The door was closing on some skinheads in white tee-shirts, suspenders trailing down the sides of camouflage fatigue pants. The tables were covered with paper plates and the remnants of chocolate cake. While Amy and I worked, the others had been partying, but the party had moved out into the late morning sunshine. Amy skipped down the steps and out the door. I followed slowly, drawn by curiosity but restrained by fear.

From the nearest porta-cabin, a two-way stream of men went in and out. Those coming out carried rifles. One of the kitchen help, the pasty-faced, stringy-haired girl, was carrying a box that said Remington. She followed the rifle-bearers down the pathway to the firing range behind the barn, where she sat on a bale of hay and doled out bullets like Halloween candy.

The men were forming a straggly line in the center of the rifle range. They were a ragtag bunch that would have made George Washington's early conscripts look like an award-winning drill team. One of the skinheads had cocked a knee to support his rifle while he pulled up his suspenders. The gun had gotten entangled in the straps, and he was swinging it around, trying to free it. Those near him were not amused.

This was my first view of the whole group, including the ones who'd arrived during the morning. There were about twenty guys (some were too young to be called men). Half were skinheads, like the ones I'd seen with Dwayne at the Old Republic. Others, including Erich, Mitch, and Zane, had hair—but really short hair. Dwayne's hair wouldn't have rated a second look in any setting, except it was red. All of them were wearing the same steel-toed combat boots. I was the only one who hadn't fetched himself a rifle.

About a dozen females were sitting on the hay bales with the ammunition-girl. Most were making coarse jokes about the inept militia trying to line up in front of them. A thin, fragile-looking girl was patiently holding a rifle for one of the older men, while he adjusted his clothing. Another woman, cigarette hanging from her lips, was actually standing behind her man, pulling his suspenders in place and tucking in his shirt.

Jerrod was near the far end of the line, on the left. He was staring at his rifle while hefting it, like he was testing its weight. I had no idea whether he was an old hand at guns or not. We'd never talked about it. He was positioned next to a tough-looking skinhead who looked to be completely at ease with his gun. With his rifle-butt resting on one combat boot, he was shaking his head and sneering at the antics of his fellow corpsmen. "Jesus," he muttered.

"Jesus," came a loud, deep, theatrical voice from behind me, "would drum this pitiful band of soldiers out of his army, if he could see them now."

A muscular man came striding up. He had a heavy mustache, eyebrows that almost met above the bridge of his nose, and shaggy, dark hair blowing back from a high forehead. His face was bright red, leaking energy from the Texas sun back into the environment. It was the man in the upstairs window, the "just a guy" who comes and goes and is the only person who can tell Bea what to do.

"Stop all that fidgeting and line up. A straight line, for God's sake. . . . Bea!" He whirled back to yell at Bea Nichols, who was straining to catch up.

"I'm coming, I'm coming."

"What in hell have you brought me? I've never seen such a miserable excuse . . . you!"

It took me a second to realize he was now shouting at me. When I did, I jumped like he'd hit me with his fist.

"Why are you standing there? Where's your rifle?"

"I . . . I'm just here to . . ."

Bea spoke up, between gasps for breath, "It's okay, Robert. He's the Spanish translator."

Robert turned to Bea. "So?"

"So, he just got here. We haven't talked about anything with him. Not yet."

"What's your name, boy?"

"Peter. Pete."

"All right, Peter-Pete, why don't you take yourself back to the house. Maybe little Ms. Nichols will be so kind as to talk to you about things later."

Bea jerked her head toward the house, her face dark with anger.

As I walked away, I heard the man saying, "All right, now Peter-Pete's gone, let's try it again, pussies. For those who don't know me yet, my name is Robert Gaither. Not Bob, not Robbie, Robert. You might want to remember that. Now, look left and form a straight line . . . left! I said left. My God, Bea, if we gotta rely on this bunch of lard-asses to save this country, we're in deep . . ."

"This is the first time he's ever talked to us." Carrie Bell found me in the mess hall, idly poking at scraps of chocolate cake left strewn on the table. "Usually he just talks to Bea. He's the head of the organization, at least around here, I think. There's others in town that don't get out here much, but I don't know them." She walked behind me and started massaging my shoulders. "I don't really know a lot."

My mind was in a turmoil, trying to process everything I'd seen that morning. I wanted to ask Carrie all sorts of questions, but the massage was getting to me, siphoning off my energy. I settled back, let her rub away, and said nothing. When her right hand strayed from my shoulders and tiptoed down my chest, I flinched. I oughtta stop this now. What kind of guy am I, to let this happen? Besides, I had a girlfriend. The old-fashioned phrase, "being unfaithful," came to mind. But was I being unfaithful, letting Carrie do her stuff? After all, I couldn't even remember what we'd done at the party in the woods. Is it wrong if you only think something might have happened? Carrie wasn't and never would be my girlfriend. There wasn't, and never would be, any emotional attachment between us. She was just this person, this thing, really, doing pleasant things to my body. What was the harm?

Then the picture of some guy, some thing, rubbing his hands all over Jennifer's chest, struck at me like a fist coming out of the screen at a 3-D movie. I jerked away from Carrie.

Seeing the hurt on her face, I said, "Hey, Carrie. I don't think Bea'd like the idea of the troops getting too friendly."

"Lots of the troops are friendly. Even Dwayne's friendly." She almost spat out her last words.

She reddened and turned away. So that's it. Carrie's been all over me, but it's Dwayne she's thinking about. Carrie is jealous of Elaine Wilson.

I didn't know what to say, but the sound of the door saved me from agonizing very long. It was Zane. He stopped in the doorway when he saw Carrie and me. I could tell from his face he was certain he'd interrupted something. He rocked back and forth, as if he couldn't decide whether to come in or retreat.

I said, "Hey," grateful to have my little session with Carrie ended.

"Hey," said Zane. He slipped into the mess hall with his head down and his body turned to one side.

Carrie started for the door, but stopped in front of Zane, square on, with her hands on her hips. "Baby, he's all yours." Then she stalked outside, slamming the door behind her.

"Did . . . did I . . . were you . . ." Zane stuttered.

I just shook my head. "Why aren't you out playing soldier?"

"I wasn't doing it right, I guess. Mr. Gaither said . . . he said a . . ." Zane looked at the floor. "Nothin'. Forget it."

"Hey, c'mon. It's bugging you bad, so tell me."

Zane shook his head, continuing to look at the floor. I put my hand on his shoulder. "Tell me."

"No," Zane shouted, pulling away.

"Tell me."

"He said . . ."

Zane's voice dropped to a whisper. "He said, in front of everybody, a baby like me can't be trusted with a gun."

"In public? He called you a baby?"

"Yeah. And did you hear Carrie? So did she."

"Aaah. That was different."

"Was it?"

"Yes, it was. Look, how come you let everybody walk all over you? Even your buddies. Mitch treats you like dirt."

"No, he doesn't."

"Yes, he does. You don't even realize it, do you?"

"He's my friend."

"He calls you names. All the time. In front of other people, too."

Zane sat across the table from me and turned to look out the window. "Friends call each other names."

"But with you, it's all one way. You'd never call Mitch a name, would you?"

"He might not like it. Besides, it's just words. He never hits me."

I was quiet for a minute, wondering where that had come from. I decided to prod gently. "So, a good friend is one who doesn't hit you?"

He nodded.

"Who's hit you?"

Zane shook his head.

"C'mon, Zane. Talk to me. I'm okay."

Zane mumbled, "My dad."

"Your dad hit you?"

"And other stuff." Silently, he turned away and lifted up his shirt. His back was covered with round scars—burn scars.

Oh, shit," I said.

"From when I was small." Zane pulled himself up and tried to get himself under control. "Anyway, now I don't ever go home if I can help it."

"I guess I understand. Being afraid all the time would be rough."

"But you don't understand. I'm not so much afraid of him anymore as of me. I'm afraid I'll lose it and . . . and kill him."

"Jeez. What's your mom say about it?"

"She always takes his side. Said if I was better, he wouldn't have to do it. 'Course, he beats up on her, too, and she says the same thing about herself. Says she always brings it on herself."

"That's tough, man." I thought about my own mom. She'd watch me being abused for about two seconds, then somebody'd be hauled into court, or they'd find themselves out in the street on their ear, scratched and bleeding. I thought of the way she'd hissed at the cops threatening her kitten at the police station. I said, "Let's go for a walk."

"Where?"

"Upstairs. Everybody's outside, 'cept you and me."

"I don't think that's a good idea."

"C'mon. This is your chance."

"To what?"

"To show you're not a baby."

The stairs went halfway up to a landing, made a one-eighty, and continued toward the front of the house. There were several rooms behind closed doors—probably bedrooms. Behind us was an open door. We went through it into a huge room, which took up the entire back half of the house. It was set up auditorium-style, with rows of folding chairs facing a podium and a blackboard. The walls were covered with posters, flags, and blown-up photographs.

The flags were mostly Stars and Stripes, but one was a Confederate flag, and two were pure white with black swastikas. The photos were of groups of people posing for the camera in front of other posters and flags. Some were wearing white robes and a white peaked hat—Ku Klux Klan obviously. The robes of two of the men weren't all white. They had black bars sewn on the ends of their sleeves. A black sash was tied around their waists, with the ends trailing down their sides almost to the ground. They must have been the head guys. In another picture, a bearded man, holding a microphone, was dressed in a shiny blue robe and a tall conehead hat shaped like the pointed dome on top of a Turkish mosque. I was pretty sure he wasn't an Islamic clergyman leading the faithful in prayers.

I can't say I was surprised at what I was seeing, but the way the whole room was filled up with it, it was overwhelming. It was powerful. It was also very, very scary.

After I'd recovered some of my composure, I pointed at one of the posters and asked Zane what it meant. It was a drawing of a man standing with his arms and legs spread wide, with a circular laurel wreath behind him. The man's face was totally white, totally blank. No eyes, no nose, no mouth.

"That's the 'Faceless Aryan Warrior,' " said Zane.

"I've seen some of the skinheads wearing tattoos like that," I said. "What's it mean?"

"It's supposed to be the guys working by themselves, without any leader. Guys no one knows about—that's what the blank face means—doing what has to be done for the white race. That's a German victory wreath behind him. Means he's gonna win, before he's through. That's what they told me, anyway."

I snorted. "The Nazis lost the war, if I remember my history."

Zane shrugged.

There were a lot of small posters, with sayings like "White Power," "If I Had Known This—I Would Have Picked My Own Cotton," "It's a White Thing!" "God Created Adam and Eve—Not Adam and Steve."

I had just started around the room to read the posters when I heard noises from downstairs. People were tromping into the house, shouting and laughing. We froze as the rhythm and volume of sound increased, coming closer. The crowd was on its way up the stairs—the only way down and the only way up—to where Zane and I stood immobilized.

CHAPTER 11

ANE TURNED ALMOST AS WHITE AS THE Faceless Aryan Warrior. He bolted for the door. "C'mon."

"Wait. Too late."

"But Gaither'll get really mad."

"You run downstairs now, you'll look guilty."

"I feel guilty. I am guilty."

The thunk-thunk of heavy boots on the stairs shook the floor.

"Sit," I told Zane, as I threw myself into a chair near the back of the room. We were both seated like good little schoolboys when the first bald-headed patriots came through the door.

"Lookie here. It's Peter-Pete and the babe."

"Ain't that sweet."

"Skinny Peter likes babies, seems."

Laughs.

"Seems Babe likes skinny peters."

More laughs, and the heavy thud of combat boots on the wooden floor, as the troops marched themselves to chairs near the front of the room. The women straggled in and sat behind their men. The scraping of chairs, shouting, and horseplay made it feel like a class whose substitute teacher had stepped out into the hallway to regain sanity. As Bea Nichols and Robert Gaither appeared at the door, I looked at Zane, nodded, and smiled. Zane's worries about getting caught were over. We were just part of the crowd.

When the "class" noticed Bea and Gaither, the noise level subsided. Within seconds, the room was silent. Bea took a seat in an oversized chair in the left front corner. Gaither stood in front, dead center in front of the podium, and faced the assembly.

"Let me repeat," he said, "what I mentioned so gently outside." Then he shouted, "Y'all are the piss-poorest excuse for a militia I've ever seen. And believe me, I've seen some piss-poor ones."

He started to pace right to left and back again.

"You think this is a game? A video game? You think, when the final days come, and you're confronting the enemy—you think you can just push the reset button? Game over—play again?"

Most of the guys in front sat rigid, staring straight ahead, even when Gaither wandered far off to the side. A few were squirming, apparently finding their chairs suddenly uncomfortable. Two of the younger women leaned together, whispering and snickering. They soon found they'd made a mistake, as Gaither marched to a spot just behind them, grabbed each by an arm and pushed-pulled them to the front of the room, opposite Bea, and ordered them to stand without talking throughout the assembly.

"Not one word. Understand?"

"Yes," said one of the women.

Gaither leaned in to her until his nose was almost touching hers. He shouted, "Last I heard, 'yes' was a word. I want no talking. None. Do you understand?"

She was bug-eyed with fear. Her mouth opened and closed, fish-like. Another "yes" was certainly about to pop out, but she managed to close her face down, tuck her chin into her chest, and nod, using her whole upper body.

Gaither went back to the center of the room and smiled at the group as if nothing had happened. "Boys and girls," he said, "it's time for our study of Scripture. Bea, who's got the study guides?"

The next half-hour was surreal. Gaither led the troops in a convoluted journey through the Bible, picking and choosing passages which he claimed "proved" Jesus was a white man of the same stock as those who founded Germany and the Scandinavian countries, tracing his ancestry from Adam to Noah to King David.

Adam and Eve, Gaither said, were the first white people, but not the first people. "The Bible is very clear on this. Adam's name comes from the old Hebrew 'aw-dawm,' meaning 'showing blood in the face,' which means having a ruddy complexion. Clearly, Adam was white, 'cause dark skins don't show red."

One of the women raised her hand. "Sir?"

"Yes."

"So where do the dark-skinned people come from?"

"Very good question, young lady. You see, it says on the sixth day, God created men—not man, mind you—men, plural. Then he rested on the seventh day—before the Garden of Eden or Adam and Eve are even mentioned. Those were the mud people, the dark races, God created on day six. He didn't create white people until after he'd rested and given it some more thought." He laughed, like he was enjoying a private joke. "Guess after a good nap, He decided He could do better."

Gaither went on to lead us through the study guide's chapter on Noah. "People think Noah's family was the only one on earth to escape the flood. Not true. They were the only white family to escape. You know why?"

No one volunteered.

"Because, they were the only white people who weren't screwing around with dark people. They were the only ones keeping the white race pure."

He raised his arms like he was embracing the whole room, and his voice took on the dramatic quality of a revivalist preacher.

"That's why you, my friends, are so special. That's why you . . . have been chosen, chosen above all others to do God's work on earth today. The flood tide of destruction is upon us, even as I speak to you. But this time the earth will be cleansed, not with water but with fire. The white fire of God will destroy all but the righteous, and the white ashes of the damned will fly in the wind."

Many of Gaither's flock had pushed forward and were sitting on the edges of their seats, their faces lit. I expected many of them to leap to their feet at any minute and shout, "Alleluia," but Gaither continued to speak. He paced even faster, punching the air with his fist for emphasis.

"Look around you. White men fornicating with the devil. White men cohabiting with mud people wherever you look, mongrelizing the race. Mexicans, everywhere, the ultimate mongrel race, the product of white Europeans lying with the Indians they found living brutish lives in the New World.

"And who am I? Who do you see, standing in front of you? I am the new Noah. I am the new Noah, and you . . . you are my family, God's chosen people."

The room was silent. No "Alleluias," no talking even. I looked around and saw everyone seemed mesmerized by what they'd heard. One of the girls who'd been made to stand at the front of the room looked like she might burst into tears. Gaither went to her and wiped her cheek with his fingertips, slowly. She glowed with pleasure. Then she pressed her lips together and clamped her eyes shut.

Gaither led her back to her chair and motioned for her companion to sit, too.

"And now," he said, returning to the front of the room, "it's time for us to plan our next steps. It's time for the next phase of God's plan to cleanse the world with fire. This will be a dramatic demonstration of our will—a far more spectacular . . ."

Gaither drew back as Carrie Bell jumped to her feet and rushed toward him. He leaned forward again, however, when she cupped her hand next to her mouth to show she wanted to whisper something. He listened, then scanned the room until he spotted me near the back. He patted Carrie with the back of his hand, and she went back to her seat, throwing me a quick, venomous glance. Gaither, still staring at me, called for Amy to come forward. The two of them stood with Bea and whispered for several more minutes. Then Gaither said, "I've just been reminded of the importance of time in our next phase. Amy has prepared documents that require immediate release to the Spanish-speaking community. Amy, please take your assistant, Peter . . ."

"Grayson."

". . . Peter Grayson, to the communications center, while the rest of us continue our work."

As Amy and I left the room and went down the stairs, I dragged myself along as slowly as I could, trying to hear what Gaither was saying about the next "phase." I could only make out a word or two—"devices," "explosives," "trucks," and Amy was at the bottom of the stairs, urging me to hurry.

At her computer, she started working on an address list. She stopped and handed me a CD.

"Put your 'Warning' file on this and give it to me so I can attach it to these emails."

"Who are you sending it to?"

"Everybody in town we could find with a Hispanic surname. Or something in their profiles that shows they're spics. There aren't all that many. Guess they're not that wired. It figures."

"Why the hurry?"

"I don't know. Gaither says to hurry, so we hurry. Something about that guy, Councilman Ruiz, going out of town—a boondoggle, Gaither says, whatever that is."

"Why do we care if he leaves town?"

"I dunno. Except he's the most important one for this message to reach. We need to scare the hell out of him, says Gaither, and we gotta do it now."

I put the CD into the computer and then sat back. So far I hadn't done anything except put some words on paper. But the minute this "Warning" document goes out over the Internet, I'd be involved. There'd be no way to pull it back. I'd be one of them, one of this loony-bin collection of hotheads and crazies. I know I'd promised Jerrod I'd help him spring Elaine, but I couldn't go any further. It was crunch time.

"Hurry up, asshole."

"I . . . I can't."

"What?"

"I can't do it. This isn't my thing. I won't."

"Jesus. Get out of the way. I'll do it."

I pushed her back, ran the cursor up to Edit, Select All.

Amy shouted, "Noooo," as I stabbed at the Delete key, then Save. She tried to bat my arm away, but it was too late. Every word I'd struggled to interpret was instantly gone. Amy and I watched the blank screen in silence, then she got up and left the room, not saying a word.

I wanted to run into the hallway, out the front door, and as far away from the Nichols Ranch as I could get. But what would be the use? I had no wheels. They'd catch me on the road in a minute, and I could hardly walk for miles across open fields with the cattle and the fire ants. Better stay and take what comes.

What came was Robert Gaither, bounding down the steps at full speed. He bounced off the doorway making the turn into the computer room, his face even more "aw-dawm" than usual. It was bright red, flashing danger.

"You little shit! You got no idea what you've done."

I just shook my head.

"No stomach for it, huh? I knew it the minute I laid eyes on you." He stamped and whirled, alternately lowering his chin to his chest and turning the whites of his eyes to the ceiling. "Dammit. I knew it. I knew it. Knew I should have refused to take you, even if it was orders."

"Whose orders?"

"Never mind." He turned back, clenching and unclenching his fist, his whole body rigid with anger. He breathed hard for a minute, but gradually the clenching and the breathing slowed. He stared quietly, then nodded. He said, "Maybe this'll be better. Maybe you did us a favor."

"Wha . . . What?"

"Why should we warn old Ruiz? He's had plenty of warnings."

"Of what?"

"Of what happens to beaners that're in the wrong damn country. That's what. Especially now."

Gaither walked to the door, then turned back. "There's going to be fire, a cleansing fire like you've never seen. The final campaign to rescue white America is about to begin, and the first blow will be struck right here, right here in Bennington."

He started to leave, then whirled back again, a huge grin on his face. "And the enemy will never see it coming. They are about to die, but they don't know it. Thanks to you, Peter Grayson, thanks to you."

CHAPTER 12

I WAS FLAT ON MY BACK ON A CHENILLE-COVERED twin bed, staring at the weary whirl of the overhead fan. The pale blue curtains hung limp at the window, which had been fastened shut with a set of heavy screws. I'd discovered this while watching the last of the visiting army marching single file out the front door below me. In the parking lot, they scattered like refugees from a kicked ant-hill, then disappeared, one-by-one, into their pickup trucks. A late-model sedan, probably the Eldorado, moved to the far end of the parking lot and stopped. Porch lights glinted off of its shiny black shell. Pickups clustered around it, like ants again, tending their queen. One of the trucks suddenly sped off alone. At one minute intervals, the others followed. The queen, her eggs ejected, returned to the ranch house and parked below me. Gaither got out and walked slowly into the house.

With nothing but my mind to occupy time, I was in pretty poor company. I thought about prisoners of war, isolated in darkened cells. I thought about Romanian orphans, sitting blank-faced in cribs, denied touch, speech, or sight of anything outside their tiny rooms—from birth. I shuddered.

I sat upright when I heard talking in the hallway and a key in the lock. The door burst open and Jerrod exploded into the room, propelled by Robert Gaither's powerful shove. The door slammed shut and relocked, while Jerrod pulled himself off the floor slowly and, it seemed, painfully.

"Hey, Pete," he said.

"Hey, Jerrod."

"Thought you might like a touch of company."

"You thought."

"I s'pose it got thought for me."

"You all right?"

Jerrod didn't answer. He just stared at the floor for a while, then shook his head.

He looked up sharply. "Ya know? Everything was fine, till you went and showed up. I was doin' all right."

"I didn't just show up. They brought me here. Said I'd come if I was your friend." Watching the scowl on Jerrod's face, I felt anger pushing up from somewhere deep inside me and into my throat. "You're the one's to blame. You and those stupid medals."

"I told you why . . ."

"You should have told me from the start! You should have told me about Elaine. Should have asked me if you could use the medals. We were friends!"

Jerrod kept staring at the floor.

I said, quietly, "At least I thought we were. Guess not."

Jerrod turned his face to the side and looked at me. "Truth?"

I shrugged. "Truth."

"I think I was kinda mad at you."

"Mad? Why?"

"'Cause of Jennifer. You started in hangin' with her all the time. I felt . . . like a house dog in an outside kennel, I guess."

Whoa. I'd thought she was being silly, telling me Jerrod was jealous. Turns out her woman's intuition was spot-on, and my male blinders were effective as all hell. I wondered what else I'd missed. Probably lots.

"Sorry, guy. You gotta believe me, it wasn't intentional. I never meant . . . I wasn't dumping you or nothing. It's just . . . well, Jennifer . . ."

"It's okay, Pete. The real reason I couldn't tell you was 'cause my sister's here. Besides, we got lots worse to think about."

"You got that right. Look . . . tell me why they were suspicious of you."

Jerrod walked over to a closet door, opened it, and looked in. "Empty."

"And why you're in here with me."

He pulled open the drawers of a chest, one at a time, and slammed them shut. "I thought old man Gaither was stayin' in this room."

"There was a suitcase sitting on the bed when they shoved me in here. He took it."

"Guess he's a-movin' on."

"Not till they do what they're planning to do in Bennington. Jerrod, we gotta get out of here. Now tell me, how did you get on their shit-list? Why are you in here?"

Jerrod stared at me with glistening eyes and down-turned lips pressed thin. "My sister," he said, finally. "Elaine did it."

"Did what?"

"When I first got here, she stayed clean away from me. Wouldn't let me talk to her without other folks hangin' round. Finally, the other day I caught her alone. I almost got on my knees, begging her to give this up and get herself on home."

"What'd she say?"

"Threw a fit that'd make a hornet look cuddly. I told her how Mom and Dad were worried sick. Then she started to laugh. Said why did I think she'd come here in the first place."

"Like she was running away from home?"

"Something like that. Said she was sick of my getting everything I wanted while she had to beg. Dad giving me the Firebird was the last straw, so she said."

"How'd you answer that?"

"Hell, how could I? Said I didn't think Dad meant to treat her worse'n me. Said she oughtta come on home so he could make it up to her."

"And?"

"She laughed again, kinda wild-like. She said there was no way I could speak for Dad."

"I always thought she was spoiled rotten. Instead she's jealous of you. Go figure."

"Yeah."

"What makes you think she ratted on you?"

"'Cause Dwayne came to see me just a few minutes after Elaine went stomping out. He grilled me really hard 'bout why I was here. I gave him the same old shit about 'the cause' and all that. He didn't believe me."

"Probably 'cause you didn't come off as believable. Neither do I."

"So here we is."

"Jerrod, something really bad's being planned, and it's gonna be worse because of me."

I told him about the document I'd destroyed, keeping them from sending it to the Hispanic community. I told him about Gaither's ominous conclusion that it was all for the best, and their message would be delivered all the more forcefully without any warning.

"Warning about what?"

"Explosions. Fire. 'Cleansing' fire, he said. And the main target's going to be one of Bennington's City Councilmen. A Hispanic guy. Probably others."

We heard the key turning in the lock, and fell silent as the massive form of Bea Nichols entered the room. She was back in her buckskin phase. The soft blue butterfly had crawled back into its overstuffed brown cocoon.

She clucked her tongue and shook her head. "You boys, you boys. I am so disappointed in you, and in Dwayne, for not seeing through you."

"Gaither said I was here because of orders, not because of Dwayne—or you. Who's really giving the orders? Is it the guy that was behind Gaither in the upstairs room when I got here, trying to keep out of sight?"

"Not your concern."

"There's some phantom hiding in the background, pulling your strings, Gaither says there's something really nasty planned for us, you got us locked in a room, and you say it's none of my concern?"

She shrugged her massive shoulders and turned to go.

I gathered my courage and asked Bea, "What about you? How'd you get to be the way you are?"

She whirled back. "I've always been this way. Whatdya mean?"

"I mean all this business about Hispanics and Blacks and Jews. And the evil government. That stuff."

Bea's eyes blazed, and she took a step toward me. I stepped back.

"When my husband was alive—before he was murdered by your precious government—I let him do all the work, all the planning. I was the little housewife."

I almost laughed at her ludicrous choice of adjectives.

"I stayed at home and cooked and sewed like all the other women, while he went out to his meetings."

"How'd he . . ."

"They killed him. Claimed he was stockpiling weapons for a holy war against the Hee-spanics and the Black people. When he wouldn't give the guns up, they surrounded the house. Shot him. The bastards."

"So you took over?"

"Someone had to. Dwayne was still too young. In the end, I decided I liked being in charge."

"So you're like one of the officers in this war you keep talking about, against the . . . the African-Americans and the Spanish-speaking people and . . ."

"Why do you call 'em by these fancy new words? Call 'em what they are. What we always called them."

"I was taught those words . . ."

"Bullshit! We gotta watch our tongues, talkin' about them, but they can call us names—whitey, honky, goyem, gringo—and we just sit back and smile."

"'Cause we've never been oppressed."

"They killed my husband! You think I never been oppressed?"

For a brief moment, I felt a flicker of sorrow for the big woman. She was shouting at me, but her eyes were filled with pain. I started to say I was sorry for her loss, but she cut me off.

"They will pay. They will all pay. And you two, young men, will be the sparks that light the fires of the coming of the end."

Bea swirled out of the room and slammed the door on my feeble protest.

Jerrod said, "Good goin,' Pete. You really smoothed things over with the old lady."

I wasn't listening to Jerrod. My mind was still on Bea's last words. Not only was something horrific going down, but these people had reserved a place for Jerrod and me, right in the center of things. We were going to be "the sparks that light the fires."

"Jerrod?"

"Yeah?"

"You know how in Africa they sometimes stake a small animal out so the lions'll come and eat it, and the hunters have an easy shot?"

"What're you getting at?"

"I got a feeling we're gonna be the ones staked out."

CHAPTER 13

WE HEARD SHOUTING IN THE HALLWAY. I recognized Gaither's deeply resonant voice. The door opened a crack and remained there, held by a hand whose fingers gripped the edge while their owner continued to argue. Only then did I realize the other voice belonged to Dwayne Nichols. He was pleading, almost whining, "Leave her alone, Robert. She ain't done nothing."

"Not yet. But she will. Trust me. Blood is thicker . . ."

The door was pushed open, and Elaine was shoved into the room, in much the same rough way Jerrod had been. And me. After the door closed, it was quiet for a few seconds. Then we heard the sounds of laughter as Gaither and Dwayne retreated noisily toward the stairs. So much for Dwayne's protests about Elaine. Just show. Another performance in a deadly circus, where even the clowns carried weapons and the audience was not expected to leave the tent alive.

Elaine was crying. Through her sobs she showered Jerrod and me with the foulest language she could drag up. If we hadn't shown up, she would still be happy with Dwayne, not imprisoned in a room with us.

"Dwayne doesn't give a damn about you," said Jerrod.

"Yes, he does. Yes, he does. He loves me."

"Bull. He loves to have sex with you."

Elaine threw herself at Jerrod and tried to scratch his face. He held her off, and she ended up punching wildly at his arms.

"Sex and love, sis. Two whole different things."

"No. No. He said he . . ."

"The dirtbag said what he needed to say to get your bones in the sack."

Elaine screamed and lunged at Jerrod again.

He said, "Didja hear him just now, laughing his ass off in the hallway? Did that sound like a guy who loves you? Two different things, sis, two different things."

Elaine collapsed into her brother. He wrapped his arms around her, and the two of them stood silently shaking, while I retreated to a corner of the room, embarrassed to be witnessing all that raw emotion.

Jerrod didn't let me disappear, though. He called out to me, "Am I right, Pete, am I right?"

Images of Jennifer raced through my mind, superimposed with the feel of Carrie Bell's fingers straying down my chest. I nodded, more to myself than to Jerrod, then said, "He's right, Elaine. For guys . . . sometimes it can be two different things."

"It shouldn't be," she sobbed.

"I know it shouldn't, but sometimes it is."

I moved away from the two of them and started searching the room, looking for anything that might help us escape. The screws holding the windows in place were set deep and hard. Besides, even if we got out that way, there'd be a long drop to a concrete slab right in front of the door. Too risky.

"You think we'll get out of this?" Elaine spoke up, from where she had curled up on the bed.

"Have to think so."

She started crying. For the first time since I'd met her, I felt an emotion toward her other than disgust at her nose-in-the-air attitude. Takes a crisis, I thought, for people's full character to show itself. She'd always treated me like I was crud under her fingernails. I was about to ask her if she still felt that way, when we heard cars and voices outside. I asked her, "What would you have done if you'd stayed with Dwayne, and you'd found out what he was doing?"

She pressed her lips together and stared at the wall.

"If you'd found out what he was planning to do?"

Silence.

"You don't know, do you?"

Elaine sniffed, and tossed her nose upwards—some of the old Elaine showing through.

"Elaine." My voice was hard. "Do you know what these people are? Do you know about Epstein's farm? Didn't you know . . ."

"Stop," she shouted. "No, I didn't know."

"But you must've suspec . . ."

"I didn't want to know. Can't you understand, I was wanted, I was . . . loved."

Jerrod spoke up. "You was used."

Elaine started to flare up at her brother, then she pulled back into herself. She nodded, almost imperceptibly.

"Look," I said. "It's no use going over and over this same stuff. We've all been used. Time for that later, when we're out of this."

"Yeah, right," said Jerrod, sarcastically.

"Yes, that is right. I'm afraid we don't have clue one about what's gonna happen, so we got to plan for different contingencies." I turned to Elaine. "That means different possibilities."

"Asshole." Aaah, the old Elaine.

Elaine walked to the window. Without turning, she said, "I suppose it will be all right. When our parents realize you two precious boys are missing, they'll have the cops out here."

Jerrod sighed. "Mom and Dad know about the ranch, but they don't have a clue about where it is. What about your mom, Pete?"

"Thanks to Bea, she thinks I'm somewhere on Galveston Island getting a suntan."

Elaine came back to face us. She seemed perfectly composed now. She said, "So you didn't tell anyone about this place?"

Jerrod shook his head.

I said, "I didn't know anything to tell."

Elaine strode to the door and knocked once. The door opened immediately, and Dwayne pulled her through, grinning wickedly over her shoulder.

Elaine said dryly, "We're clear. Nobody knows a thing."

Jerrod cried out in anguish and threw himself at the door, but not in time. It closed with a decisive thud, and the lock was thrown. Jerrod leaned against the door, mourning the sister he'd lost in more ways than one.

CHAPTER 14

OOK WHAT I FOUND. HELP BOOST ME UP, JERROD. I think we just got lucky."

While Jerrod lay immobile on the bed, shaken by Elaine's betrayal, I had searched the room looking for anything that might help us escape. I'd looked briefly into the closet and was about to close the door when I glanced at the ceiling. There was a small square panel surrounded by molding. It was probably a door into the attic.

Jerrod ignored me, so I called him again. With a groan, he pulled himself off the bed and walked across the room to the closet. I told him to lace his hands, and I stepped up. I rested my elbow on top of a shelf to take some of the pressure off Jerrod, who was grunting with the exertion. When I pushed up on the square of wood, it moved easily, and I slid it sideways to reveal a dark space. I could just make out rough wooden beams slanting above.

"Push me up. Now."

I pulled, and Jerrod pushed, complaining with every painful inch. Finally, though, I had my shoulders and both arms through the hole. I hung, trying to gain strength for the final pull. Jerrod had let go, and my legs were swinging free.

"Last push, Jerrod. Get your shoulders under my feet, then shove up."

"Your shoes are gonna hurt."

"Just do it, Jerrod. Shut up and do it."

He did, still grousing. With one motion, I hauled myself up and rolled to the side. I found myself lying precariously on a narrow beam, a two-by-six, with my elbow pressed into the splintered wood. Other beams were spaced about two feet apart, disappearing into the darkness. Attic heat, dust, and an oppressive musty smell made it hard to breathe. I was shaking from the exertion and the discomfort of my narrow perch. Carefully, I got into a crouching position, steadying myself with a hand on one of the slanting roof beams above. There wasn't enough room to stand. Moving around was going to be a bitch.

Of course the real problem was, where was I going to move? If the crawl hole I'd just used was the only way in or out, there was little reason to be up there. There were bits of light at intervals around the edges of the attic, probably ventilation holes, and certainly too small for me to get through. Toward the back of the building, though, beyond where I assumed was the meeting room, there was a patch of brighter light—a larger hole. Maybe it would be big enough for me to fit through. I moved, slow as a tree-sloth. I had no desire to stick my foot through the ceiling and into some-one's startled view. In fact, all it would take was for someone to hear me, and I'd be busted.

I sneezed and then froze. Wouldn't it be crazy if I got caught because of some microscopic dust particles? I didn't hear any noise or talking from below, so I started my journey again. When I finally reached the source of the light after what seemed like hours of painful crab-crawling, I found the hole was large enough for me to get through, but it was covered by a grate. Through the wire mesh I saw a small sloping porch roof and chocolate-cake-strewn tables beyond. The hole was just above the steps leading from the original house into the mess hall. No one was in sight, so I jerked at the grate, risking some noise. Little by little it loosened and, with a satisfying retching sound, pulled out of the hole. The way was clear.

I waited a while, to be sure no one had heard the noise, then carefully slid myself out onto the tiny porch roof. It was steeply sloped. There was no way to hang over the edge to let myself down gently. Once I let loose of the hole in the wall, gravity was going to do the rest. I angled myself to where I hoped there were no tables, laid on my back, took a deep breath and let go. As my feet slid over the edge, I jack-knifed upwards so I could see what was ahead.

What I saw was the bottom step of the porch. There was no way I was going to miss it! Pumping the air with my arms, I managed to get the weight of my body in front of my legs but didn't have time to plant my feet where I needed them to be. One foot hit the step solidly, but the other glanced off the edge. Instead of rolling into a clean forward somersault, I twisted sideways, fell on my side and ended up scattering chairs and wrapping myself around a table leg.

The noise was awful. I was shaking from the fall and from fear of discovery. I wanted to curl up under the table, but decided soon enough it wasn't a good plan. It was only when I tried to stand I felt the pain in my heel where it had caught the step. There was a soreness in my ankle, too, that I knew from experience was going to get worse. Much as I hurt, I had to move quickly.

Hauling myself up the steps, one at a time, I remembered watching Bea raising her ponderous bulk on the same journey the day before. She'd managed it with more grace than I was showing. Inside the door, I ducked into a little alcove under the stairs and stopped to listen. Television sounds floated down the hallway. I tiptoed ahead and realized that, if I was to make it up the stairs to rescue Jerrod, I would have to pass in full view of the living room. I peeked in carefully and saw the back of Bea's shoulders and head. Dwayne was in one of the side chairs, but angled away from the door enough so I thought I could get by without discovery.

Then I heard it. The knob on the front door was turning. Whoever was coming in would see me down the hallway the second the door was open. I ignored the pain and hobbled back as quickly as possible to the alcove under the stairs. I huddled against the wall as footsteps approached, quickly at first and then more cautiously, leaving no doubt in my mind the newcomer had caught a glimpse of me. I decided to step back out into the hallway in hopes I wouldn't look so suspicious. I'd pretend I was looking for something. When I did, I met the startled look of Zane Weathers. He stopped and backed up, his mouth working silently but wildly. His eyes danced from me to the living room and back again, in a frenzy of indecision.

I put a finger to my lips, silently pleading with him not to give me away. I could see in his face he was agonizing over his loyalties to Mitch and the others, and to the newfound friendship I'd offered him. He took one more long look into the living room, then smiled nervously and nodded his head at me. I felt relief flooding my veins.

I'd just started to move cautiously forward again when Dwayne's voice cut through the TV's background noise. "Zane. What's goin' on?"

Zane jerked. His body appeared to be moving in all directions at once. He seemed on the verge of running back to the front door, but then he stood facing me with grief painted all over his face. He raised a trembling finger and pointed at me.

"It's him," he croaked. "It's Pete. Right there. He's right there."

CHAPTER 15

OUR NEW PRISON WAS ONE OF THE PORTA-CABINS. As darkness fell outside, I realized, with relief, we now had one big advantage over our upstairs room in the house. We had a bathroom, with a small toilet. I cringed at the thought of having been stuck in that room with Elaine, with no facilities. I tried to imagine what I'd have done—or what she'd have had to do, for that matter—if we'd stayed upstairs. She'd solved part of the problem by bailing on us. Still, I was trying to convince myself spraining my ankle and bruising my heel had been worthwhile.

For hours, I'd been seething with anger at both Elaine and Zane. I can't say I was surprised at Elaine's treachery, although her Academy Award-caliber performance was a revelation. But Zane. I'd given Zane the promise of friendship without strings, of sympathy for all the crappy things he'd had to endure, and hope for a way out of this life of being the butt of jokes at the hands of his so-called friends. When the shit hit the fan, though, he'd panicked.

Then I had a new thought. If I were Zane, if I'd had to endure all the crap he had, would I act any differently? The more I thought about it, the less sure I was.

"Jerrod?"

"Yeah?"

"What do you think of Zane?"

115

"Now? Or before he chickened out and squealed on you?"

"Before, I guess."

"I felt sorry for him. 'Course, he brought it on himself, letting people jerk him around like that."

Jennifer had said almost the same thing about me once, a million years ago. I can be like a dog, she'd said, who puts his tail between his legs and lets people kick his butt. Am I really so different from Zane then? Compared to Zane, I feel way superior—but is that just my ego talking? I thought about all the things in life I refused to get into—team sports, for instance—for fear of failure. That's not being superior. That's being chicken.

"D'ya think Zane feels sorry for what he did?"

"Not so sorry," Jerrod said, "as how he'll be if'n I get hold of his scrawny neck."

"I been thinkin' about that. Let's not be stupid. If I read Zane right, just about now he's feeling really, really bad for what he did. If he is, it might come in handy before we're out of this."

I didn't say the same thing about Elaine. For one thing, it almost certainly wasn't true. She wasn't sorry for a thing. For another, his sister's behavior was just too painful for Jerrod to think about. It didn't stop my mental ramblings, though. What would she do when she finally had to face the reality of what her boyfriend was up to? When the killing started, would she stay with him? As different as she was from her brother, they were raised in the same house with the same values, weren't they?

Car doors were slamming every few minutes. I peered through the blinds to see if I could tell what was going on. Several of the vehicles in the parking lot had their lights on, and dark silhouettes floated in front of them. Some of the figures carried boxes to the backs of pickups, then returned to the porta-cabins. Every ten minutes or so, one of the pickups would roar into life and peel off down the road.

I said, "They're taking off one at a time, so they don't look suspicious pulling out onto the highway. Whatever's going down, it'll be tonight."

Jerrod stood beside me. "So, Einstein, have you decided what we're gonna do?"

"I don't know what's happening or where. And I really don't have a clue how you and I are going to figure in it. We've just gotta keep our eyes open and be ready to jump if we get the chance." I hobbled around the room, trying to keep my ankle flexible. Every time I sat it would stiffen, and it was hard to start moving again.

"Jeez, I hurt. If we get to where we have a chance to take somebody down, you're going to have to do most of the work, Jerrod."

"I'm not much of a fighter."

"I'm not, either. Give him a knee where it hurts."

"That's easier said than done, I think."

"Then keep your eyes open all the time for something you can grab. A stick, a lamp, a rock—anything. Grab it quick and whack him on the head. Look, I know this all sounds kinda silly. But I still think it's a good idea. We have to keep our minds sharp, thinking all the time."

Jerrod went to the window to watch the proceedings in the parking lot. There was a new confidence in his step. He didn't look beaten down by fear, like before. I felt the same. Maybe all this talk about fighting back was just stupidity, the improbable stuff of Hollywood action flicks, but it was already having an effect. If we were going to face death, we were going to do it with our eyes open and our brains working.

"I think they're about through," said Jerrod. "Hard to tell, but I think there's only a couple of cars left."

Sure enough, seconds later, a key turned in the lock and the door crashed open. Robert Gaither stepped into the room, holding a shotgun. He was dressed completely in black. His grinning red face was the hourglass on a black widow's abdomen. Hope was sucked out of us like the guts of hapless insects bound in a web of fear. As Gaither advanced across the room, Jerrod and I froze. Our brave talk of struggle and escape died in our throats.

CHAPTER 16

AITHER DIDN'T SAY A WORD. HE MOTIONED to the door with his shotgun, then prodded Jerrod and me in a quick-step down the walkway to the parking lot. My ankle throbbed, but I tried not to let it show. I stubbornly refused to let Gaither see any sign of weakness, even though I was shaking with pain and fear. A line from some movie flashed into my mind, about brave men not being fearless; they just kept going in spite of their being afraid. I didn't feel the slightest bit brave, but I wasn't going to let anyone in on that little secret.

Floodlights at the corners of the house illuminated a semicircle of empty parking lot and glinted weakly off chrome and paint on the dark fringes of gravel. The piercing rays of headlights angled away from the house, deepening the blackness beyond.

Someone unseen shouted, "You're next, Bill. Take off."

A pickup roared into life, fishtailed a few times on the gravel drive, then caught traction and sped off into the night. Only two cars remained, the Eldorado and Jerrod's Firebird. Jerrod was ordered into his car, and I was told to sit in the front seat of the Cadillac. I waited while Gaither conferred with three people standing next to Jerrod's car. I thought about jumping out and sprinting to safety, but gave it up almost immediately. Even without a bad ankle, there was little chance of reaching the darkness, and the open fields provided no cover.

I felt a stab of guilt, too. Jerrod was still trapped, and he was probably feeling worse than me. He'd come on a mission to save his sister, and he'd failed completely. Then I had another thought. What about the people in town, Councilman Ruiz and the others, who had no idea of the destruction that was heading toward them in the backs of a convoy of pickup trucks? Crazy as it sounds, their only hope lay with a couple of boys they'd never met, two boys who had yet to see their seventeenth birthdays. Maybe we never will.

I tried to picture my mom, sitting in front of the television with her dinner on a tray, thinking her son was enjoying Spring Break with friends at the beach. I wished I could make some psychic connection with her, like Spock and Captain Kirk, but what could she do anyway? Just worry. I couldn't tell her what was going to happen or where, since I didn't know myself.

Gaither strode to the door of the Eldorado and handed his shotgun to someone, who jumped into the seat behind me. It was Dwayne. Gaither searched his pockets for keys, started the engine, and turned toward Dwayne and me. "Well, boys and girls, this is it."

He accelerated smoothly down the drive. As we left the parking lot, he nudged me with his elbow. "Didn't your parents teach you anything, Peter-Pete? Fasten your seat belt. You ought to know riding without a seat belt isn't safe." He laughed, and I cringed at the implied menace in his joke.

It took us close to an hour to get into Bennington. A handful of late-night stragglers made their way home from restaurants and bars, busy with the business of living. They had no idea death had just rolled into town.

On Main Street, people were coming out of the Cimmaron Palace Theater in groups of two and three. One couple stepped off the curb ahead of us and crossed the street, holding hands and laughing. As we passed, the lights on the marquee went out, and we could see an usher standing in the doorway, waiting to lock up behind the last of the customers. Gaither motioned to the darkened theater and said, "Well, there it is." Dwayne grunted.

We turned right and drove a block to the town square. The white frame of the octagonal bandstand was just visible in the dark. Gaither circled the park slowly, looking right and left at each corner and constantly checking his rearview mirror. "Looks good," he said, turning into a familiar alleyway, the narrow space where I'd first seen Mitch emerging from the Old Republic bar. I soon learned that the bar's side door was our current objective, too, as Gaither braked abruptly and Dwayne jumped out. He threw open the passenger door, unbuckled my seat belt, and hauled me out of the car. Gaither was already starting to move as he shouted, "You know what to do, Dwayne. See you in the morning." Dwayne slammed the door shut, and Gaither tore off into the night.

"Inside," Dwayne said, prodding me with Gaither's shotgun. We groped our way down the same hallway as before, past the same restrooms reeking with beer and urine and vomit. The bar was dark and empty, but the smell of smoke was still strong. Clearly, the last of the customers had staggered out the door not long before.

Dwayne pushed me through the back door into the courtyard, and into a surreal scene, dimly lit by a single bulb attached to the back wall of the bar. Dark figures huddled around boxes stacked against the far wall. Others stood or lounged in groups of two or three. They were talking quietly, but there was an unmistakable tension in the air.

In contrast to their companions, three of the group were laughing under the green and white awning. Two of them were pulling cans of beer out of the cooler and handing them to one of the younger skinheads, who was stretched out on top of the bar, with his elbow pressing into a flat cardboard box wrapped in Christmas paper. Dwayne paused for just a second, then lurched into action, grabbing the skinhead by his shirt front and throwing him to the ground.

"You assholes!"

"We was just . . ."

"Shut up. Put the beer back and get outta there."

While Dwayne was occupied, Jerrod and I were left alone at the door. Jerrod whispered, "C'mon, let's split."

I whispered back, "What about Elaine?"

"You heard her. It's no use."

"I don't think she really knows what she's into."

"Maybe not," said Jerrod, "but there's nothing I can do about it now. Let's go."

"I still can't run. My ankle. You go for help."

Jerrod hesitated, then turned back to the door.

Dwayne's voice cut through the gloom. "Don't even think about it!"

Jerrod and I turned back to face the barrels of Dwayne's shotgun once again. We'd let our chance slip away. Dwayne called for some rope, and one of the group rummaged around until he found some. When he ran up to hand it to Dwayne, he kept his face turned away. It was Zane.

Dwayne jerked the rope away and thrust the shotgun into Zane's hands. "Watch them, while I get 'em tied."

Forced to look at us, Zane seemed really miserable. This time it was my turn to look away.

Jerrod and I were tied, hands and ankles, and propped up against the rear wall of the Old Republic, where we had a clear view of what was going on. Very little was. Gradually, the small groups scattered around the courtyard stopped talking and people curled up on the dirt to sleep. A few sat with their backs to the wall and smoked. Every once in a while someone would get up, stretch, and amble into the Republic. I guessed they were using the restroom.

I desperately needed to go, too, but I delayed saying anything because the person who had been charged with guarding us was a woman. I couldn't hold off any longer, though, and she called to one of the smokers to help me.

"Shit," he said, throwing his unfinished cigarette into the dirt and crushing it with his foot. He untied my feet and started to prod me toward the door. Then he stopped and hit his forehead with the palm of his hand. "Shit again," he said, glancing at the front of my jeans. He untied my hands. I wanted to laugh, I almost laughed, but the laugh caught in my throat. The toilet-from-hell lay in front of me and a gang of ruthless racist murderers was at my back.

When I'd returned to my place against the wall and the ropes were retied, I found the last of the cigarettes had been stubbed out and the smokers had joined their companions on the ground. I counted twenty-four in all. Jerrod was snoring, still propped up against the wall. I stretched out on the hard ground and tried to empty my mind so I could sleep. I wanted to be in shape to deal with whatever was going to happen in the morning, but I couldn't stop thinking. I kept playing and replaying every possible scenario for what might lie ahead, my ankle was feeling even worse, and the hard ground fought against the pressure of my hip bones. Still, I was surprised when I heard the sound of voices and opened my eyes to a square of blue sky trying to throw the light of a new day into the shadowy courtyard.

CHAPTER 17

SOME OF THE BOXES HAD BEEN BROKEN OPEN, and food was being handed out. I thought Jerrod and I were going to be excluded, but Dwayne told our morning guard not to tie us back up when we'd returned from another pit stop, and we were given a share of a delicious breakfast of dry but sticky bars pressed out of trail mix.

After the meal, the troops got busy. Marty and another woman removed a grate from across a ground-level window in the building opposite the Old Republic. It separated easily from the bricks, so the fasteners must have been taken off earlier. Marty pushed on the window, which opened inward, hinged at the top. Satisfied, she stood aside for Paul, one of the older skinheads. He had taken off his shirt and paraded around the courtyard flexing his abs and demonstrating how impervious he was to the morning chill. Standing in front of the window, he put his hands on his chest, stuck his chin in the air and took in a deep breath. When it seemed enough people had witnessed his performance, he snapped his fingers and a young woman hurried to him with a coil of clothesline rope. As he climbed through the window, the last thing to disappear was a bare arm, sporting a circular swastika tattoo.

The window opened again and, after some jiggling, stayed open. Paul had propped it up or fastened it with the rope. Standing inside, the window was at chest level, apparently in a basement room.

It was just then Robert Gaither entered the courtyard. He strode briskly to the window, nodded to Paul who was leaning on the sill, then turned to face the crowd. Everyone stood at attention as he spoke.

"This, boys and girls, I should say men and women, is the day we've been waiting for. All our work, the fruits of our study, will be made manifest by what we do today. Most of you are only dimly aware of our operation at the farm of old man Epstein and his illegal alien spics. We involved a limited number of you there for reasons of security, not of trust. Today that will change. Be assured, that Jew farm was a pinch of dust in the wind, compared to what we do—what we all do—today."

A low murmur passed among the troops. Several of the girls clasped their hands together under their chins, in an attitude of rapturous prayer.

"We now engage in a preemptive strike, the first great battle of the war. You are all God's chosen, the foot soldiers of the white race. Be confident in today's work. The outcome has been preordained. We cannot fail. All that is required is to do it. Are you ready?"

"Yes, oh yes."

"We're ready."

"Lead the way, Robert."

"Yes. Yes!"

Gaither stood silently while the excitement of his followers crackled around him. He held up a hand, instantly quieting the crowd, and said, "Then let's get going."

He issued orders, and his troops sprang into action. Half of the men grabbed flashlights and climbed through the basement window. The other half handed them boxes, some clearly marked "Dynamite."

"Stack them anywhere," said Gaither. "I'll be with you in a minute."

A few of the women were instructed to begin uncoiling a large spool of brown wire. The ends were connected to a box with a switch on top, which they placed just beside the door to the Old Republic.

Most of the women stood by, with nothing to do. I wondered why Gaither had chosen to bring this huge group of people to do what could easily be done by a half-dozen. Guilt. That's what he's establishing. He wants them all to be guilty in the eyes of the law. Even though he'd convinced his people they had a mandate from God, the despised authorities insisted killing people was a crime. Gaither wanted them all guilty, so none would be tempted to defect.

Jerrod and I were ignored for most of the morning. I tried to talk to my old buddies Mitch and Erich, but whenever I did they made a big point of turning away and being really, really busy. Zane looked way uncomfortable when I got anywhere near him. *You should be embarrassed, you little weasel.* Jerrod and I wandered freely around the courtyard, but were discouraged from getting near the door to the Old Republic by a rifle-toting guard. When Mitch took over the guard job, I tried to talk to him. He scowled, waved the rifle at me menacingly, and ordered me away from the door. The boy who had befriended me was gone. When I approached Erich again, he shook his fist at me and barked out, "Get away from me, Grayson."

During Gaither's address to the troops, I had quietly positioned myself by the bar under the awning. While the crowd was being whipped into a froth of patriotic fervor, I slipped open the lid of the Christmas paper box and glanced inside. It held a stack of handbills with a photo captioned "Councilman Arturo Ruiz." Afraid of being caught, I only had a chance to glance at the message, which was in Spanish, but I made out the words, "take up arms against the white oppressors."

Back against the wall, I told Jerrod what I'd found. "They want to kill the Hispanics but leave false evidence the Hispanics were planning to kill whites. Remember what Gaither said about this being just the opening battle of an all-out war? Those pamphlets are supposed to be a reason to keep the war going."

"People would know they're fake."

"How?"

"If they were real, they'd be in Spanish."

"They were in Spanish . . . Jerrod! They were in Spanish, and I didn't write them! This business about needing me to write their Spanish was another load of crap."

"So why did they really recruit you?"

I could only shake my head. Gaither said he'd been ordered to recruit me. Maybe by the phantom figure in the upper room. Maybe by someone else. At any rate, Gaither and Bea and their crowd seemed more devious at every turn.

After a mid-morning head-run, I asked my escort about the building with the basement window.

"That's the Cimmaron Palace, of course. What did you think?"

I hadn't had a clue, up until then. But now I understood why Gaither had said the fire at Epstein's farm was nothing compared to what they were going to do. They were going to bomb a movie theater, and a movie theater can hold an awful lot of dead people.

With the exception of a rifle-toting Marty, left to guard the prisoners, the entire group accompanied Gaither into the theater basement. They were gone for about half-an-hour, then reassembled in the courtyard. This time there was no talking. Gaither shook hands with two people, and they silently left through the Old Republic's door. A minute later, Gaither pointed to two others, who stepped forward with heads bowed. Gaither put his hands on their shoulders, and they looked up with weak smiles. Another handshake, and the two melted away. This solemn ceremony was repeated at intervals until only seven people remained in the courtyard— Gaither, Dwayne, Paul with the swastika, Zane looking scared, Elaine hanging defiantly onto Dwayne's arm, Jerrod, and me.

I got Jerrod aside and whispered, "What a weird bunch old Gaither decided to keep here. I can see Dwayne and that rough-looking Paul guy. I guess you and me and Eileen because he wants to make sure we're seen to be guilty as hell when this thing happens, whatever it is."

"Why Zane, though? He's such a weak character, I wouldn't think Gaither'd trust him worth a flip."

"I think I know why," I said. "It's because he's so chicken and goes along doing whatever he's told, that Gaither wants him here. Making Zane feel really guilty is the only way they can be sure he won't spill his guts if he gets in a tight spot later."

"I suppose."

Gaither looked at his watch. "It's noon. One hour to go. Until then, we wait."

Gaither and Paul leaned against the wall near the door; Jerrod and I did the same at the far end of the courtyard; Zane sat by himself, with his head resting on his knees. Dwayne pulled a giggling Elaine behind the bar, and they settled out of sight next to the beer cooler. I glanced at Jerrod's grief-stricken face and patted his knee. His face hardened, and he started to get up, but changed his mind and stretched out on the ground. He rolled away from me and faced the wall.

"One o'clock," Gaither announced. "Time to get moving."

He and Dwayne picked up walkie-talkies, and Dwayne climbed into the theater basement. They tested their communications with Dwayne moving around in different parts of the building. Satisfied, Gaither ordered the rest of us through the window.

From the window sill there was a four-foot drop to a concrete floor. We were in a small storage room, which apparently didn't have working lights, and Dwayne had to illuminate the floor with his flashlight so we could avoid a clutter of dust-covered stacked tables and folding chairs. The air was musty and hard to breathe. We followed the black electrical cord into a small, brightly lit adjoining room, empty of any furniture. The amount of dust on the floor showed this room hadn't been used, or at least cleaned, in years. There were three ways out of the room: the doorway through

which we'd come, a steep stairway leading upward, and one leading downward.

Robert Gaither spoke quietly. "From now on, there is to be no
talking above a whisper, and only then when I've asked you to.
Understood?"

His stern gaze took in all six of us, guards and prisoners alike.
Everyone nodded. Under Gaither's prodding, as usual with the
business end of his shotgun, we continued to follow the electrical
cord down into a space with a ceiling so low we had to stoop to
get around.

Elaine was giggling. "Oooh, it's so spooky." Dwayne grabbed
her shoulder roughly, and she got quiet.

"We're under the stage," Jerrod whispered. Gaither whirled
around and backhanded Jerrod across the face. Jerrod crashed
into the wall and sank down, shaking. I heard a sharp intake of
breath from Elaine, but she managed to choke it off. From the look
on her face, she'd suddenly realized this wasn't a game.

"I'm scared, Dwayne," she said, in a thin voice. He answered
with a hand poised to give her the same treatment Gaither had
given her brother. She raised her hands defensively and backed
away, her eyes bright with fear.

Gaither sent Zane for a coil of rope. When he returned, Gaither
grabbed the rope and thrust it at Dwayne. "Tie them up," he ordered.

Dwayne started to grab my arm, but Gaither stopped him. "Not
Grayson. The other two. We've got other plans for Peter-Pete." He
motioned to a vertical water pipe across the room. "Hook the girl to
that pipe and her little brother to this one over here. I don't want
them close enough to untie each other, and I sure as hell don't want
them where they can kick these here wires free of the dynamite."

He pointed at Jerrod. "Even if you could, you wouldn't be doin'
yourself any favors, kid. You try to unhook 'em, their rigged to go
off. *Bam.*"

We all jumped, and Jerrod hit his head on the low ceiling. Gaither laughed the kind of laugh that showed he was really enjoying this. He said, "Don't think I'm telling you this to save your worthless little hide, kiddo. I'm telling you this 'cause I don't want you to muck up our timing."

Elaine was crying. "You're hurting me, Dwayne."

"Shut up." Dwayne shoved her roughly against the water pipe. He tied her hands to the pipe and then wrapped a few lengths around her body. After he'd done the same to Jerrod, he went back to Elaine and put his nose up close to her face.

"Do you know why I'm so happy to see this day come? Do you? Do you?"

Elaine shook her head.

"It's because I'm finally through with you, you little slut. No more pretending. Your silly giggling and mooning eyes make me sick."

I just had a glimpse of Elaine's stricken face as Gaither pushed me back up the stairs with the barrel of his shotgun. Zane came next, looking dazed. Dwayne followed, then turned and whispered to the prisoners, "Don't try to shout. Don't even try to talk. You talk, you die. Got it?"

Dwayne listened to the silence for a minute. "That's good," he muttered to himself.

I stared at the narrow passageway that led down to where my best friend and his sister were imprisoned in a room full of deadly explosives. As I turned away to learn what "other plans" Gaither had for me, I thought I heard a faint sound from below. I thought I heard Elaine say softly, "I'm sorry, Jerrod."

CHAPTER 18

AITHER SHOVED ME TOWARD THE WINDOW. "Get your butt back outside."

Swastika Paul was waiting in the courtyard. I could see the lower half of him through the window. When I started to climb through, he grabbed me by the armpits and hauled me out. I ended up in the dirt on hands and knees, not knowing whether I wanted to stand up or curl into a ball like one of those roly-poly bugs. Paul settled the matter by shoving the sole of his boot against my side, sending me rolling.

I decided to lay there and watch while Gaither and the others climbed out of the building and huddled in conversation. Occasionally, one or the other would glance over at me and nod his head. I was torn between fear for what they might have planned for me and worry about Jerrod and Elaine down in the chamber of horrors.

Paul was sent back inside to keep an eye on my friends. Dwayne and Zane sat against the wall while Gaither sauntered over to me. He checked his watch.

"They ought to be getting here soon. It's almost time for our special screening."

"Who?" I stammered.

"That Councilman Ruiz guy and the other beaners, that's who. They're having a meeting upstairs in the Cimmaron to discuss

130

the fire out at Epstein's and a few other little problems they been having."

"Wha . . . What are you going to do?"

"We're gonna give 'em another little problem. 'Course they won't be around to worry about it." Gaither threw his head back and laughed.

When he'd finished, I worked up the courage to ask him, "Why am I here?"

"Good question, Peter-Pete. Ya see, there's not going to be just spics up there in that theater, there's going to be white guys, too. Your job is to get the white guys out the door and keep the brown guys on the stage."

I shook my head. "But why me? Why can't you do it?"

"And show my pretty face? I don't think so."

"How am I supposed to separate them?"

"You're a real big talker. We've seen that. Here."

He handed me one of the brochures from the Christmas box. "Give this to one of the white guys. You know one of them. That fellow your mother works for."

I must have had my mouth hanging open, because he said, "You don't think we picked your name out of a hat, do you? Now listen good. You bring this here box of pamphlets up the stairs and put it on the stage. Then you take Langer aside, and you show him one a these brochures. Convince him he oughtta call all the white guys outside to discuss it, before the spics learn what you've got. Dwayne will be watching from the stairway. When you're out, he'll let me know." Gaither patted his walkie-talkie.

"Why wouldn't I . . ."

He screwed his face up into a chilling excuse for a smile. "Thass right. Your little buddy and his sis. They stay tied right where they are until everything upstairs is just the way we want it. Just the way you are going to make sure it is. Right?"

I nodded dumbly.

Gaither looked at his watch again. "They're in the building now. We'll give 'em fifteen minutes in case some of them's late. They got a whole different sense a time than we do. Fifteen minutes, then we move."

I sat against the wall like the others, but as far away as I could get. My mind was reeling. How in hell did I allow myself to get into this? I was just being a good friend, I decided. Instead of telling the police how I loaned my Nazi medals to Jerrod, I went chasing after him. Yeah, right. Why not try admitting some oversexed female stuck her tongue in your ear and you headed off into the wild unknown hoping for more? No, not fair. It was Mitch and Erich and Zane. They came along just when everyone else was giving me hell. How did I know what I was getting into? How was I to know what kind of crazies they all were?

If someone had been watching me, they'd have seen me look to the blue oblong of sky with a pained grin on my face, then drop my chin to my chest and struggle to keep from crying.

You knew. You knew, didn't you, Grayson? Maybe not the details, but you knew they were no good. You didn't know they killed the family at the Epstein's, but you could sure as hell have guessed, if you'd wanted to. You're as bad as them. You admit you don't have any Hispanic friends, or Black friends, or . . .

Now they're going to make sure you're one of them. Not only that, they're going to make sure everybody knows you're one of them. In a few minutes, you're going to be a murderer, unless . . . unless you can pull yourself together and put that brain to some use.

First thing to do is figure out what Gaither is really going to do. He and Bea and the whole bunch of them have lied every which way they could. Is there any reason to expect them to be telling the truth now? Maybe, maybe not.

The explosives in the basement are real enough. I've seen them with my own eyes, and the detonator is right over there. Got to figure they're going to use them, because they've killed before. Got to figure it's true enough they expect me to get any white people out of the building before they blow things up. How about Jerrod and Elaine, though? How about me?

They claim they're waging a war, but they sure as hell aren't going to come out and publicly admit they did it afterwards. They may be "soldiers," but I'll bet my life they plan to keep fighting their war from the shadows.

The minute I thought of the phrase, "bet my life," I felt ice water flooding through me. How were they going to let Jerrod, Elaine, and me live through this? Live through it so we could identify everyone who had a part in this?

"It's show time." Gaither dragged me to my feet and shoved me toward the basement window of the Cimmaron Palace Theater. I'd run out of time to plan any way out of this mess. In a minute I was going to climb the stairs onto the stage. Then I was going to have to decide whether to save all the people up there and condemn my friends to certain death, or to grab onto whatever slim chance there was of saving myself by sacrificing the others.

CHAPTER 19

THE STAIRS TO THE STAGE WERE STEEP. The treads were barely wide enough for my feet, and I wasn't able to watch them anyway. The pain in my bad ankle was excruciating, and I had to hitch myself up one stair at a time, leading with my good foot on every step. The heavy box I was carrying didn't help. I was looking up at Dwayne, who was standing at the top with his walkie-talkie hanging from his belt and a finger to his lips.

Gaither had whispered last-minute instructions at the bottom of the stairs. "Don't forget, boy, the box goes on the stage near the table where the big-shots will be. Take out one of them flyers and show it to your guy Langer. After that, it's up to you. Get the white guys out, keep Ruiz and any other of his high-mucky-muck Lat-tee-no friends on stage. Soon as you do, Dwayne'll give me the signal and the two of you get your butts back down here."

The stairs came out at the side of the stage near the back, behind some curtains. Dwayne pulled me around to the side of the curtain, and I could see the whole auditorium. There was another curtain up front, but it was pulled back to the sides. I wondered where the movie screen was, then saw it hanging way up high in the dark, above the lights. It seemed every light in the place was on.

There was a big folding table on stage with six people sitting facing the auditorium, where there were maybe a dozen people in the first two rows. Someone banged a gavel on the table, and everybody got quiet. When the head guy started to speak, I didn't hear what he was saying because my head was whirling around with my own thoughts.

He knew! Gaither knew exactly how things would be set up, with a table on stage. He just told me to talk to "my guy Langer," so he knows my mother's boss is one of the city councilmen and that he'd be here. There was no time to think about that, though. Dwayne gave me a shove in the back, and I walked out onto the stage with a stupid-looking Christmas box in my arms.

The man with the gavel was talking excitedly and shaking his finger in the air when he saw me. There was dead silence as a couple of dozen eyes followed me out onto the stage. Gavel-man had dark hair and skin the color of the oak dresser in my bedroom. I guessed he was Ruiz. Two of the other men at the table looked Hispanic, too. The others were white, and I saw one was a woman. Maybe she was on the city council, too.

My mom's boss, Councilman Mark Langer, was on the far end of the table, and I heard him say, "Peter! What the devil are you doing here?" I expected him to sneer at me like he always did, but instead he seemed almost glad to see me, despite his surprise.

I didn't answer right away. I put the box down, pulled out a flyer, and asked Langer if I could talk to him. When we were away from the others, I said, "This is going to sound weird, but hear me out. There are some crazy nuts, white supremacists, I guess you'd call them, who are planning to blow up this theater."

"What?" Langer's eyes hardened, then darted around the room.

"Please listen to me. They've got people tied up in the basement right next to the explosives, and if I don't do as they say—if you don't help me—then they're gonna get blown up."

"You're joking."

I shook my head. "There's a whole bunch of these flyers in that box. When the place goes up, they'll be found. The flyers are supposed to make people think the Spanish-speaking people like

Councilman Ruiz are planning something really bad against white people. But . . ."

"Are they?"

"No! These are fake. Gaither's gang made them up themselves."

"Gaither's gang?"

"Yes. I'll tell you about them later, but now we gotta do something—quick."

Langer squinted his eyes and wrinkled his brow. "So what do we do?"

I was hoping Langer would have a bright idea, but it didn't look promising. He was still squinting and wrinkling and shaking his head slowly.

I said, "Someone's watching from the back of the stage. If it doesn't look right, he'll bolt for the door and give the signal to set off the dynamite."

"Good Lord."

"You're supposed to call all the white people on the stage and in the audience to go out into the lobby to talk about these handbills, like you believe the Hispanics really wrote them and you need to figure out what to do."

"And you?"

"I've got to go back downstairs so they'll let my friends loose."

He nodded and pressed his lips into a thin smile. "That's really admirable. You're mother will be so proud of you."

I choked up on that. "Trouble is, I don't think it's going to work that way. I think my friends and I are going to get killed anyway. We know who these guys are."

We stared at each other for a long time. I could hear two people at the table talking quietly in Spanish. Spanish!

The answer came to me in a flash. "I know what to do now," I told Langer. "You get all the white people outside, just like I said.

Then I'll talk to the Hispanics. I can speak some Spanish, see? The guy over at the stairs with the walkie-talkie won't know what I'm saying."

"What will you say?"

"I'll tell them to wait till you're out, and until I've gone back down the stairs, and then for all of them to run like crazy."

"It'll never work."

"What other chance do we have?"

"You'd have to get all the way back down the stairs, untie your friends, then out through the window into the courtyard. You'd never make it in time."

"Still . . ." I swung around to stare at Langer. "How did you know about the courtyard?"

His face twisted in sudden rage. He grabbed my arm and pulled me roughly toward the back of the stage.

"You're gonna ruin everything, you little turd. Mother's precious little boy. If she didn't wait on you hand and foot, maybe she'd save a little for me."

"You're one of them. You're the guy behind Gaither. Upstairs."

"Brilliant piece of deduction, kid. Maybe you can figure out just who brought you into this operation. In a couple of minutes, you'll figure out why."

Dwayne materialized out of the shadows, and Langer shoved me toward him. "Take him down, now."

I turned and shouted as loud as I could, "Get out. There's a bomb. Everybody out."

Dwayne fumbled for the walkie-talkie as I threw myself at him. The walkie-talkie went flying, and I crashed into Dwayne. We fell back into the stairwell. I heard Dwayne bump down the stairs and thwack into the floor below, while I clutched desperately at the top of the handrail.

I could hear excited voices and people running. Langer shouted, "Damn you, Grayson," and then he was running, too. I steadied myself and then climbed painfully down the stairs. Dwayne was on his side, moaning. I found the walkie-talkie and threw it hard against the floor to make sure it was broken.

I ran through the storage room and started down the lower stairs to where Jerrod and Elaine were imprisoned.

"Not so fast." The words slammed into me from the rear.

I spun toward the window to see Gaither's shotgun pointed at my chest.

"Let's go, Peter-Pete. I don't know what all happened upstairs, but you shouldn't be here, since I haven't heard from Dwayne. Ease yourself on out here now."

I crawled out through the narrow window and into the bright sunshine. Gaither called to Zane and ordered him to get upstairs, find Dwayne, and learn what was going on.

"Don't do it, Zane," I called. "Help Jerrod or he's **dead**."

Gaither started toward me, and Zane threw me the same helpless look he'd given me in the hallway of Bea's house, just before he'd betrayed me to Dwayne. I didn't have time to think about it, though, because Gaither swung the butt of his shotgun, and I felt a sharp pain and saw a constellation of brilliant lights that slowly faded to black. I didn't quite lose consciousness, but I found myself on the ground with my cheek pressed into the dirt.

"Do as you're told, Zane. Don't you listen to this greaser-lovin' piece of trash. Now get going."

When Zane had gone, Gaither muttered, "Knew that stupid kid was getting to be a goddam liability. Shoulda just tied him up with the others right away instead of stringing him along trying to make him useful."

I expected Zane to be back as soon as he found Dwayne lying at the bottom of the stairs. When he didn't return, I started to hope maybe he'd screwed up the courage to listen to me instead of Gaither. I tried to ignore the pains in my head and ankle and figure out what to do next.

Gaither barked, "Paul, see what's takin' so long."

Just as Paul reached the window, Elaine's head and shoulders appeared. Zane had come through! Paul stopped short. Elaine came bursting through the opening, propelled from behind, with Jerrod scrambling after.

Gaither shouted, "What the hell?" He started toward the detonator box.

"Dwayne's in there," Paul yelled.

Gaither stopped and turned, then shook his head. "Can't help it."

By now I was on my feet, trying to find my balance. When Gaither swung back toward the detonator, I hurled myself at him. This time the pressure was on my bad ankle, and I buckled before I could get up any speed. I crashed into the ground and reached out to clutch at Gaither's legs. I managed a handful of cloth and felt him dragging me across the dirt. As I did so, my body twisted this way and that. I saw Paul, Jerrod, and Elaine sprinting for the far wall. Zane was halfway out of the window.

Gaither broke free and threw himself at the detonator box.

I shouted, "Nooo," just before I saw a flash of light behind Zane. Everything around me went into slow motion. Zane came tumbling toward me through the air like a rag doll. I felt the roar and a whoosh of sound rushing past me. The bricks facing the theater rippled and swelled and then cascaded down, a red-brown waterfall.

I caught a flash of brown out of the corner of my eye a fraction of a second before something struck my head with an agonizing blow. The thought *not again* flashed through my mind, but almost immediately the thought, the pain, and everything else were gone.

CHAPTER 20

FLOATING IN PEACH-COLORED LIGHT. A gentle murmur of voices. My eyelids too heavy to open. The drone of voices too comforting to try to understand. I drifted off again.

I awakened to the sound of far-off clanking. Something metallic. I listened for it again, but there was only silence. Above me, white acoustic ceiling tiles surrounded a recessed fluorescent light. To my left, blue light streamed in through a window, and I could see the tops of trees out of the corner of my eye.

There was a dull pain on the right side of my head. I was in a high bed with a railing, and beyond it my mother slept in an orange hospital chair.

"Mom," I said quietly.

Her head came up like a shot, and then she was hovering over me. "Oh, Peter." She was crying now. "I was so scared."

"Mom—what happened to the others?"

"How is your head? Do you hurt."

"Some. What about Jerrod? What about all the others?"

"Where does it hurt? Is it a sharp pain? I'll get the nurse."

"No! Mom, please. I need to know."

Mom stared out the window for a minute, then said, "Your so-called friend Jerrod and his sister are fine. A couple of others weren't so lucky."

"Unlucky how?"

Mom shook her head.

"You mean—dead?"

She nodded.

"Who?"

"Somebody named Nichols and a young boy named Zane something."

Zane.

"Mom, I need to be alone for a while."

"You're crying, Peter. Where does it hurt?"

I wanted to lash out at her; instead, I said quietly, "I'm not crying for me, Mom. I'm crying for someone else, and I've got to do it alone."

As she got to the door, I called out, "Mom?"

She turned back.

I said, "Thanks."

"What for?"

"For being you."

Jennifer and Jerrod came together.

"So you two are speaking to each other," I said. "Find some common ground?"

"That would be you, I think," said Jerrod.

Jennifer leaned over and kissed the part of my forehead that wasn't covered with a bandage. "You look good," she said.

"You look like you're gonna be auditioning for *Mummy III,*" said Jerrod.

"How's Elaine holding up?"

"Not so hot. She sits in her room and won't talk to anybody. She feels ashamed of the way she made herself horizontal for ol' Dwayne. And she's screamin' furious with him for using her like he did. 'Course, she's ashamed of that, too, on account of he's dead."

I was quiet for a minute. "Are we in trouble, Jerrod?"

"We? Everybody's saying you're some kind of hero. The guys you warned at the meeting in the theater—they want to give you a medal or something."

"No way. It was a medal got me into trouble in the first place. I wonder what Officer Prescott thinks about it now."

"He's cool with you. We had a long talk, and they know about the medals, 'bout how you got out to the ranch, the whole dang thing."

"And you?"

"Not so cool, but I'll be okay. They're after my folks for letting me go out there 'stead of telling the cops I'd given the medals to Mitch. Councilman Ruiz is saying he understands families and how my folks had to try to protect their daughter. Probably they'll listen to him, 'cause he's the one Gaither and all wanted to blow up."

I said, "The doctors said the police can talk to me this afternoon. I've got to tell them about Councilman Langer."

"They know. Turns out Robert Gaither wasn't such a hot-shot warrior-type after all. When they grilled him under the lights, he spilled his guts. Guess his face got even redder than usual."

"His aw-dawm face."

"His what?" asked Jennifer.

"Never mind. Private joke. Not a funny one, either."

Jerrod got up and headed for the door. "Methinks it's time for me to leave you two alone."

"You're not still . . ."

"Jealous of your woman, here? No way. You're such a big hero now, there's plenty of you to share."

I tried to throw a pillow at him, but he was already gone.

Jennifer took my hand and held it until I felt as aw-dawm as Gaither.

I said, "So, I guess you still have a thing for dogs."

"Oh, yes," she said. "Especially Rottweilers."

ABOUT THE AUTHOR

IN HIS PRIOR LIFE, TED SIMMONS ENJOYED a career as an oil company technology manager. Most of this time was spent in international producing operations, providing him with the opportunity to live and work in some of the world's most fascinating places. He developed a keen interest in the cultures and beliefs of other people and thinks many Americans would benefit from some of his insights.

Ted and his family lived in the jungles of Sumatra, Indonesia, the suburbs of London, and the desert region known as the "Neutral Zone" between Saudi Arabia and Kuwait. He has trod the ancient Silk Road in Central Asia (Uzbekistan, Turkmenistan, Kazakhstan, Azerbaijan), stood in the columned halls of the Temple of Karnak in Egypt, jostled with crowds atop the Great Wall of China, crawled through tunnels dug by the North Vietnamese during the war, and hunted butterflies with his teenage son in the mountains of Taiwan.

Ted Simmons is active in the writing community. He was Chairman of the Houston Writers' Conference in 2000, is currently Past-President of the Tallahassee Writers' Association, and chaired the association's nationwide Seven Hills Contest for Writers.

The novel, *White Heat, White Ashes,* was derived from events in the news during Ted's time living in one of the suburbs of Houston, Texas. The story is fictional; the conditions that inspired it are, unfortunately, very real.

Ted's first novel, *Sandstorm,* from CyPress Publications, was a 2006 *ForeWord Magazine* Book of the Year Award nominee.

In Ted's previous novel, *Diablo Creek,* also from CyPress Publications, then sixteen-year-old Peter Grayson and his pal Jerrod rescue a nearly drowned young Hispanic man from raging floodwaters. He refuses to give the boys any clue about the terrible place from which he's escaped.

After leaving their care, Pedro's lifeless body is found floating in the waters of Diablo Creek. Pete and Jerrod's quest for the truth leads them into a deepening spiral of danger and corruption. Will the waters of Diablo Creek claim more victims?

Windstorm

CyPress Publications proudly presents the next young adult novel by Ted Simmons, *Windstorm*.

When seventeen year-old Carter Chamberlain is uprooted from his quiet American life and moved to London, England, he fears his biggest problem will be boredom. Instead, he meets, loses, and finds again the girl of his dreams.

Because of Fiona, and her wayward brothers, he is drawn deeper and deeper into the clandestine world of Irish Republican Army terrorism, all the while trying to keep his own dysfunctional family from shattering. Carter's story moves from crisis to crisis until one last test of courage and resourcefulness is needed for his survival and that of Fiona and many innocent people.

Available in early 2009

Turn the page for a preview of *Windstorm* . . . .

Chapter 1

London, England, March 1982

THE NORTHBOUND PLATFORM AT ST. JOHN'S WOOD STATION was eerily deserted. Carter stood alone, staring at the concrete floor and absently scuffing his brand new Nikes on the grimy surface. His body wasn't moving, but his mind was flipping back and forth like crazy. He kept thinking of the friends he'd left behind in what was already starting to feel like an old movie. Tom, Daniel, Sandy. Oh yes, Sandy. For the first time in his life he'd worked up the courage to ask a girl out on an honest-to-God date, and it looked like it might turn into a long-term thing. Then Dad came home and dropped his bombshell. Tom, Daniel, and Sandy were now five thousand miles away and only lived in the movie inside his head.

Alone on the platform, Carter forced his mind back to the present. He'd stayed over at school a couple of hours to work with Mr. Graham, his home room teacher, on make-up assignments. He was way, way behind his classmates because the transfer to ASL was in mid-term. Actually, not even mid-term, because the summer break was just two weeks away. All his new classmates were cramming for finals in courses he hadn't even taken. What a crock this was. *Thanks, Dad.*

The American School in London was in a quiet suburb, where there weren't many factories or offices or things like that, so not many people got on the outbound train. Except for students like him. And thanks to his late departure, he was the only one there. The platform was dead quiet—but just for a minute.

When the train rolled in, he could hear the din while the cars were still moving and before the doors opened. When they did, the noise swept out like a violent storm. Shouting and cussing and off-key singing. Inside the train, he could see women and older people cowering in their seats, while the aisles were filled to capacity with pushing, shoving young men and boys, most not much older than his seventeen years. *Sheesh,* he thought. *I've run into rowdy kids before, but nothing like this.*

He ran along the platform searching for the least crowded car. His backpack was flumping up and down, extra-loaded with a gazillion books that needed his attention. Then the doors started to close, and he had no choice but to leap through the closest one, hoping those gazillion books didn't get caught on the outside. The force of his charge brought him up against the back of a guy in a green windbreaker who was just winding up to slug someone in front of him. He missed and fell forward, and the one he was trying to hit took a swipe at the side of his head. Down he went. A dozen voices quit cussing and singing and started to laugh.

Carter wasn't one of them. As the train lurched forward and then rolled smoothly out of the station, he watched green wind-breaker grab onto the silver pole people use to steady themselves. He was having trouble hauling himself up. It was crazy, Carter thought, but through all that, the guy was still clutching a can of beer to his chest with his left hand. He looked pretty smashed. When the fellow who'd knocked him down reached over and tried to help him stand, Carter knew he was in trouble. These were guys who got off on beating the crap out of each other and then ending up hugging and singing. He figured this guy wouldn't hesitate to beat the crap out of a stranger. No singing involved.

He tried to edge himself through the crowd, hoping to get out of sight, and hopefully out of mind, of green windbreaker. But the raucous, already-plastered-at-five-p.m. crowd wouldn't let him through.

"Lookie here. Whatcha got there, ya skinny poofter?"

Someone started to pull open his backpack. He jerked away. "Oooh, lotsa books, huh?"

"He got on at St. John's Wood. Gotta be one a them Yank swots."

"Whyn'tcha say something, Yank? Stand there with yer cake-hole open."

He tried to pull himself together and act as stoic as possible. He'd met enough bullies to know if he showed weakness, they'd be all over him.

"So who are you guys?" he said. "You all just break out of jail or something?"

It seemed like the right thing to say, because everyone around him started laughing again. One next to Carter threw his arm over his shoulder, leaned in and said, in a beer-drenched voice, "You said it, chum, so look out, ladies, we're randy as hell."

"Look out, skinny poofters, too!"

Green windbreaker was fully upright and lurching toward Carter. Just then, the train started to brake for the next station. All the inebriated louts standing in the aisle stumbled forward, and windbreaker grabbed the pole with both hands, losing his beer in the process. When the doors opened, he was back down on his knees, groping for the can and swearing like a drunken pirate. Carter slipped by him and out the door.

On the platform he ran toward the back of the train and went into another car, this time with a little more finesse. It was just as crowded, but at least here he hadn't made such a grand entrance. He worked his way toward the back, nodding his head in time to what he assumed was some sort of soccer club song. He hoped he looked like just one of the lads.

Then his newfound sense of comfort got stripped away. In fact, he stripped it away himself. In his new surroundings, it wasn't Carter Chamberlain who was getting picked on. It was a girl. Red-brown-haired, about his age. She was probably pretty, but her face was all screwed up in what he could only describe as half fear, half anger. He could see she could probably hold her own in any one-on-one situation, but this was too much. She was totally surrounded by leering, cursing, drunken louts, who were poking at her breasts and pulling at her hair.

He couldn't stand and watch this. He knew it was probably stupid to get involved, but he was still on an adrenaline high from his adventure in the other car, so he just plowed in and started to throw punches at her tormentors. Most of them missed, but some didn't, and he found himself the target of far more angry fists than he was giving out. Luckily, this bunch was every bit as drunk as the guys in the other car, and most of the fists whizzed by him completely. Then, either by accident or on purpose, they started slugging each other, and Carter was in the middle of an old western barroom brawl. He grabbed the girl and pulled her up against the door that goes into the next car and they sank down on the floor, out of range of the fistfight raging above.

She started to pull away, but then she grabbed on and clung to him. They stayed that way until the train reached the next station. Somebody shouted, "Wembley, mates!" and the fighting stopped like magic. Nearly the whole crowd cheered and lurched to the door and out onto the platform, elbowing and shoving. Outside, they started in with the off-key singing as they staggered toward the exit.

There were maybe a dozen people left in the train car. Some were business types, gripping their briefcases like they were filled with the Queen's jewels. Two were women who'd obviously been in town shopping. They were hunched over, hugging their day's acquisitions. One was an older woman who clutched her hands together to her throat. Her face was almost as white as her hair, and Carter suspected she'd looked a lot younger a few minutes earlier.

Then there was him. And the girl who was clinging to him like a winter coat. He didn't know what to do. Normally, he'd have gotten off at Wembley Park Station himself, to change to an express train that went straight through to Rickmansworth, where he lived. But he wasn't about to do that this time, for two reasons. One, he wasn't about to get tangled up with that gang of soccer hoodlums that just got out. Second, he had a pretty, red-haired girl squeezing her arms around him and dripping big fat tears all over his chest.

Other Books by Ted Simmons from

Cy**P**ress
ublications

Sandstorm
by Ted Simmons
© 2006 Ted Simmons
6x9, 140 pages, trade paper
ISBN: 978-0-9776958-4-3
$13.95
Publication date October 2006

A *ForeWord Magazine* 2006 Book of the Year Award nominee

DIABLO CREEK
by Ted Simmons
© 2007 Ted Simmons
6x9, 168 pages; trade paper
ISBN: 978-0-9776958-7-4
$13.95
Publication date November 2007

From the author of **Sandstorm**, a *ForeWord Magazine* 2006 Book of the Year Award nominee

To order a single copy, send check or money order made out to CyPress Publications in the amount of $19.50 ($13.95 + $1.05 tax + $4.50 shipping/handling) to P.O. Box 2636, Tallahassee, FL, 32316-2636. For multiple copies to the same address, add an additional $16.00 per copy (cost of book + tax + $1.00 shipping/handling). Please be sure to specify the title(s) ordered and the address for shipping.

Printed in the United States
203507BV00007B/1-105/P